As If

As If

ISABEL WAIDNER

HAMISH HAMILTON
an imprint of
PENGUIN BOOKS

HAMISH HAMILTON

UK | USA | Canada | Ireland | Australia
India | New Zealand | South Africa

Hamish Hamilton is part of the Penguin Random House group of companies
whose addresses can be found at global.penguinrandomhouse.com.

Penguin Random House UK,
One Embassy Gardens, 8 Viaduct Gardens, London SW11 7BW

penguin.co.uk

First published 2026

001

Copyright © Isabel Waidner, 2026

The moral right of the author has been asserted

Extract from *Molloy* by Samuel Beckett, reproduced by permission of Faber and Faber Ltd

Penguin Random House values and supports copyright.
Copyright fuels creativity, encourages diverse voices, promotes freedom
of expression and supports a vibrant culture. Thank you for purchasing
an authorised edition of this book and for respecting intellectual property
laws by not reproducing, scanning or distributing any part of it by any
means without permission. You are supporting authors and enabling
Penguin Random House to continue to publish books for everyone.
No part of this book may be used or reproduced in any manner for the
purpose of training artificial intelligence technologies or systems. In accordance
with Article 4(3) of the DSM Directive 2019/790, Penguin Random House
expressly reserves this work from the text and data mining exception

Set in 14.2/17pt Fournier MT Pro
Typeset by Six Red Marbles UK, Thetford, Norfolk
Printed and bound in Great Britain by Clays Ltd, Elcograf S.p.A.

The authorised representative in the EEA is Penguin Random House Ireland,
Morrison Chambers, 32 Nassau Street, Dublin D02 YH68

A CIP catalogue record for this book is available from the British Library

ISBN: 978-0-241-77918-7

Penguin Random House is committed to a sustainable future
for our business, our readers and our planet. This book is made from
Forest Stewardship Council® certified paper.

'And in the midst of those men I drifted like a dead leaf on springs, or else I lay down on the ground, and then they stepped gingerly over me as though I had been a bed of rare flowers.'

Samuel Beckett, *Molloy*, 1955

I

I was in no state to meet anyone when Korine arrived. I sat on a chair in my sublet on Aldersgate Street, central London: an epic Hail Mary. Outside it was tipping down. It was mid to late May. Colder than it should have been for the time of year. Distended sash window to my right overlooking an alley, or to be exact, the external wall of the neighbouring building. Water was running down black brick. Splashing out of the gutter pipe. This was the moment Korine chose to put in an appearance, I judged him on that. He walked in through the front door like he owned the place. He was taller than me, and lankier, and that's saying something, given that I myself had a hard time maintaining my posture on my chair: hard-plastic shell, cracked red with other, bleaker tones, thought-up as if for people half my height. I corkscrewed my lower legs, it gave me no comfort. How could it: Korine positioned himself directly in front of me, leaving puddles on the floor: grey marbled linoleum tiling, laid in the sixties I guessed, surviving wave after wave of gentrification.

I defaulted to common courtesy: I invited him to sit down on the empty chair facing mine like an open house.

He couldn't possibly, Korine said. His thoracic cage was prone to concussing. It hurt when he sat for too long in any one position. He would prefer to lie on the sofa. He had taken a liking to it: its teak frame, greenish leather cushions, slit where it hurt.

Please, I insisted. The chair. I was trying to contain him. Shows what I knew.

He obliged reluctantly. Sat there with his legs crossed, arms wrapped round his torso, moments from falling in on itself I was led to believe. At a guess, he was in his late forties. Younger-looking, if I took myself as a benchmark. He had dark brown hair not unlike mine, wavy and a little too long. My unremarkable eyes, they were looking back at me. He wore a novelty t-shirt, the less said of it the better, and pyjama bottoms. Not to mention his sliders: why, in this weather. Were we ever to be seen together, I thought, we would reflect badly on each other.

'Lewis,' I said as per introduction. 'Aubrey Lewis.' Former actor whose career has come to nothing, I didn't say. Husband who lost his wife and subsequently himself, I didn't lead with that either.

'Lindsey Korine,' he said. 'Pleased to meet you.' Then he said he was cold.

What did he want me to say. Weren't we all. I showed him the cream-coloured tracksuit bottoms I was wearing, the mismatched top, which crucially I'd tucked in to protect and keep warm my pelvic girdle. A musculoskeletal vulnerability, I explained, perhaps to show him it could be done: tolerate the conditions. I went to the lengths of displaying my footwear: brown Oxford shoes, oddly puffed up, pillowed, even, as if the leather had been soaked in order to swell it. I didn't know who made such things. What sort of factory. What sweatshop, it was unimaginable.

'Can we turn on the heating,' Korine said. His clothes would never dry at this rate.

'No,' I said. It was spring. The communal heating had been turned off.

Korine, I learnt, was unable to put up with his discomfort for even a minute. He got up from his chair, which was an undertaking. Nothing was simple with him. He made for the crowded coat stand by the door, minded to layer up.

Over two years into my subtenancy, I had yet to go near the various pieces of outerwear deposited there. They didn't belong to me. Hardly anything in the flat did. The paperback with the azure-blue and light brown cover on the table in front of me: I suppose it did. The cardboard boxes next to the sofa did, too. I'd never unpacked them. The flat itself, its fittings and furniture, the large part of its contents, had no connections to me or the life I had lived prior to moving here: this, the attraction. Why I had left the place more or less as I'd found it. Some concessions: my Equity trade union card on the windowsill. I once was an active member, that was before. A Kumari Burman print of a neon-lit tiger with bindis and puffy stickers of animal astronauts, a present from my wife, which I'd removed from its frame and sellotaped to the naked wall. In an otherwise impersonal environment, I had learnt to appreciate these.

Meanwhile Korine lifted one of several available tweed overcoats, grey herringbone, floor-length, and inspected it. The way he rejected it. The contempt. Not giving it a second thought, he dropped it on the floor. He pulled out a similar garment, waist-length this time: he seemed taken by it. A maybe. Still, he felt there was something better out there for him. The optimism. The leap-before-you-look sort of attitude and complete lack of self-awareness: I learnt a lot about Korine, observing his process. He threw this latest coat over his shoulder and dug deep. I felt my throat close on account of the smells released as he continued to disturb the historic arrangement: damp lanolin, decaying mineral oil, something blueberry, all in there. Korine found a scratched-up wax jacket, olive, with the corduroy collar. He tried it on. The sleeves were too short. He took that off. Returned to the waist-length tweed coat, square cut, and threw it on. It worked better in terms of sleeve length, but was too short down the torso. Still, he kept it on. He proceeded to put on the wax jacket over it. I closed my eyes and counted backwards from ten. Five. Three.

What now. Korine, in double layers, was going through one of the cardboard boxes by the side of the sofa. He selected a Christmas angel, of all things, and placed it on the table. Made out of brightly coloured foil, the thinnest of sheet metals, it was blowing its trumpet in Korine's direction. Naturally, it had its back turned on me: I was at the receiving end of its wings, the sharp edges of them, I felt insulted by that.

The turquoise and brown vase my wife had loved and I hated? Korine was holding it. He put that on the table, too.

'What are you doing,' I said, meaning don't do this.

Korine declared it was spiritually frosty in here. Bare and unwelcoming. He was fixing it.

Old tinsel: not that. Probably made of lead, I used to catastrophise. Christmas was killing us, I declared every year. Cancer, not Christmas, ended up killing Laurie. This current spring was starting to feel increasingly dangerous, too.

I can't have looked happy if Korine noticed: he held up his hands, fine, and closed the box. He promised to stop. But he left what he'd taken out of the box *out*, including the angel with the trumpet. I imagined I heard its silly fanfare.

It was madness. By which I meant, all of it. I began to entertain the idea that none of it – least of all Korine – was actually real. Why would there be anyone here: there never was, was the whole point. Likelier, I was seeing things. I had finally completely lost my mind: it had been a matter of time. I was having, what do they call it, a delusional episode. It would pass: and by this I meant quickly.

I-close-my-eyes-and-when-I-reopen-them-Korine-will-be-gone sort of quickly. Never to be seen or heard of again. I would take down the decor which I'd have to accept I'd retrieved myself while, temporarily, not with it. I would put the entire affair down as one of those things. It wasn't as if I didn't know why this was happening: against my better knowledge, I had met with the director yesterday, Fran Howe. Why go. Why do this to myself. A particularly cruel form of optimism, was why. An irrational holding on to the possibility of a comeback, if that was the word if no one noticed you'd retired in the first place. Howe claiming she wanted me, I let it affect me. She foisted that paperback on me, too. Had I accepted what I already knew, namely that my acting career was over, and so was I, Aubrey Lewis, then Lindsey Korine would never have happened.

Here we go, I thought, closing my eyes. Breathing, like Laurie had taught me. In. Out. Again, in. Out. When I look, he'll be gone.

Ok no. He was still here. Making the most of the sofa, as it were. Lying on his side, head propped up on his elbow. His legs projected out over the end of it. Restlessly, he turned onto his back – a feat, given his double layers – crossing his arms behind his head.

No good either: he sat up again. Tested the resilience of the cushioning. Made himself at home.

I'll-go-to-the-bathroom-splash-some-water-onto-my-face-and-return-to-find-him-gone quickly then. I got up and left the room. I pulled the switch in the bathroom, the light came on. So far, so good. I looked at myself in the mirror, then at the mirror itself: it was de-silvering at an alarming rate. Back at myself: my eye was a little worse for wear. My left eyelid, it was swollen. Other than that, no different than yesterday, or the day before. I washed at the sink: hands, face. I resolved to put on a towel wash later. Personal hygiene, so important. Regular things. Normal things. I straightened my track top. Fixed the tuck: I took reassurance from that.

I remembered the day I stepped into the tracksuit. This, just over a year ago. A year and a half after I quit acting. Two years after Laurie died. That day, the bathroom mirror stopped working for me: I didn't recognise who was reflected back to me as myself. The jeans I used to wear without as much as a second thought, how I resented them. The nondescript shirt. Even the belt. Especially the belt. A redeeming fact: I had taken the trainers with the N off already. I found them repellent. Next to go was the belt. Couldn't get it off quickly enough. Down with the jeans, too. Kicked them into a corner, straight off the top of my foot. Then the shirt. Off with it. Some hesitation: could I save the vest? Any forgiving qualities? Grey, formerly white. Washed a thousand times. It felt ok? No. Down with the vest. I pulled it over my head and threw it onto the pile of rejects in the corner. I consulted the mirror again. A pale long figure in underpants and, what's that, sports socks. Off with the sports socks. Hair, this was where the pins came in. I had found hairpins in the bathroom cabinet the day before: kirby grips to be precise. The original tenant's girlfriend's, I assumed. Female company. I pulled my fringe to the side, then back. Used one pin to fix it. And another. A third and a fourth. Better. Quite good, actually. After that, I went into the bedroom. Went through the various clothes that the original tenant, or sublessor, had left in the wardrobe. I chose the cream-coloured track top as soon as I saw it. Sorry no: it chose me. The beige bottoms, not a match, but close enough: I saw a possibility to relate these disparate items. I selected the Oxfords for their soft leather, unaware of their disadvantages, including a lack of ankle support: which wasn't a then problem, but more of a now problem.

Final check in the mirror: yes. A relief. I looked like someone I could bear the look of. A stranger: the best I could hope for. Long way of saying, I knew the difference a new set of clothes makes. I say this in Korine's defence.

When I returned to the living room, he was still there. Definitely, unmistakably still there. In league with the Christmas angel, heralding springtime.

2

What's your problem, Korine asks. Or, is there a problem: that.

Funny you should ask, I reply. Is there a problem: where to start.

I wasn't your typical actor, that's where. By which I mean, I come from a vastly different set of material circumstances compared to most actors I met in the industry over the decades. You'd think it doesn't matter, but it does. It means that I come at it, acting, differently. I never even thought of it as something people did until I saw Gary Oldman play Joe Orton in *Prick Up Your Ears* one night on the BBC. I was ten or eleven. I was completely arrested. I'd heard that he, Oldman, went to the same secondary school in Deptford as I did, twenty years prior, which can't have helped my subsequent overidentification with him. Seeing him on TV, I decided I would be an actor, too, but not tell anyone: growing up in New Cross, South East London, the only child to a single mother, the idea was so far removed from what was presented to me as reality it wasn't funny and was possibly punishable, Oldman, or no Oldman. I got to work straight away. You wouldn't have known it, but in my head, I was an actor twenty-four-seven and wherever I went. I'd borrow scripts from Lewisham Library, eventually all of them, alphabetically by author. I memorised lines. Absorbed language and ideas. I rehearsed entire plays in my bedroom or in front of the bathroom mirror. Neglected school homework as a result: not enough hours in the day.

What's that now. Korine getting up and walking out of the room. Me in mid-sentence. Don't mind me, I'll just talk to myself! From the bathroom, presumably, he tells me to continue. He says he can hear me just fine. I bet he wishes he'd never asked is there a problem. Hasn't a clue what he's let himself in for. Strange how I'm getting used to his presence. To him being here. Goes to show, it's good to talk. I sound like a tagline. Just Do It, too: and I did. I left school at sixteen to work in a sports shop. Trainers, primarily. An old-fashioned retail outlet, shoeboxes stacked up to the ceiling. Never the latest models. Primarily factory remainders. I didn't mind: formative years for me as an actor. 'Would you like me to see if we have these in a nine?' I'd say to a customer. Then I'd disappear round the back and check. But rather than get the shoebox down the shelf qua retail assistant, I was Hal in *Loot*, moving my mother's corpse from her coffin into the cupboard and back again. I wasn't sitting at the till on a rainy Tuesday afternoon, shop empty. I was Vladimir, waiting for Godot. That time I, as Simon from *Lord of the Flies*, played by Tom Gaman in the sixty-three film, had an imaginary dialogue with the eponymous pig's head on a stick who was in fact a customer, waiting to be served, I remember it fondly. She went on to complain to my employer, Kendall P. from Bromley: it was the intensity of my address that disturbed her. I had swayed from side to side as if in a fever dream, eyes half-closed, raving. Put the fear of god into the customer. Kendall the boss felt obliged to issue me with a warning. First and final, he said. I didn't last long after that. Which I did and didn't regret: having kept myself to myself for so long, my acting private, going semi-public on the moderate scale of the sports shop gave me the confidence I needed to take the next step.

I applied to the Royal Academy of Dramatic Art.

Feisty then. I was a feisty young thing: where did he go. Fell by the wayside somehow. Anyway, qualifications: three GCSEs and three years of professional experience. In retail, I didn't say. No matter: rejected. On the strength of my audition tape (the procurement of which was a whole other saga, involving the local library's VHS camcorder and the reluctant participation of Ms Soppo, librarian and community volunteer) they asked me to reapply next year, but advised me to find something else to do for a living. Acting was a precarious career and not for everyone. The unsubtle subtext: not for people like me. I applied to the Drama Centre in North London the year after and the year after that. No, and another no. Kept up or stepped up my informal training during this time as if in spite of it all. When I turned nineteen, I was given the opportunity to put on a public performance in an empty commercial unit in the Elephant and Castle shopping centre, now razed to the ground. Some community initiative I had applied for through Southwark Council, they let under-twenty-ones have the place for a week at a time. First time anyone, the local authority, gave me a vote of confidence. I put on a sequel to *Lord of the Flies*: the characters as nineteen-year-olds, imagined and played by myself. What can I say, people came. People watched that. My mum came. No dad, I never had a dad. Common story.

Well, I got spotted. Only in London. On the back of my *LOTF2*, I was cast in *Waiting for Godot*. Real *Godot*. Professional *Godot*. Not sitting-behind-the-till-at-Kendall's-sports-shop *Waiting for Godot*. That was big. A big step. My first-ever production was a four-week run at the Barbican, I used to tell people that. They threw you in at the deep end then. Maybe still do, I don't know. I was Vladimir, an absurdly young Vladimir, with Ekow Abduraqib as Estragon, also too young. We delivered though. Critically acclaimed, as they say. I brought something different to an industry defined by sameness, the critics said. My mum's face when I showed her the pay cheque: priceless. Kept asking how much I was paying them for the privilege of allowing me on stage. Refused to believe it went the other way: *they* were paying *me*.

I walked straight into the lead of *The Loneliness of the Long Distance Runner* after that. The production, at the National, of all places, marked forty years since the publication of Sillitoe's novella. I was twenty-one, playing seventeen-year-old Colin. Young offender, play set in a borstal in the south of

England of course. Tom Courtenay was twenty-five in the film, didn't do him any harm. On the contrary: won him a BAFTA for most promising new actor. The role was expected to do something similar for me. Help me establish myself. Instead, cracks were starting to show and god wasn't pouring into them as far as I could tell. Have you seen the internet meme, Korine? Cracks, god meant to be pouring into them? No? Not that I'm religious, not personally, no. Are you? Didn't think so. Anyway, if you really want to know whether there is a problem, Korine, listen to this: I was trotting in a circle for up to an hour every night as I delivered my Colin. Slow jog I made look energetic, tell me who else can pull this off without looking a clown. Was why, later, I tried to say it happened on account of the running. They didn't buy it. Why would they: I'd kept it up during rehearsals no problem. Not even breaking a sweat. Anyway, about two weeks into the six-week run, it was a Tuesday night, a thousand audience members watching my every move, the director and fellow actors standing in the wings, I was building up to the I-hate-to-have-to-say-this-but-something-bloody-well-made-me-cry-and-crying-is-a-thing-I-haven't-bloody-well-done-since-I-was-a-kid-of-two-or-three speech. I was working up my own tears which I had done every night including the pre-shows and several times in rehearsals, finding an easy connection to the character who decides not to win the race he is expected to win but to lose deliberately in a gesture of refusal and noncompliance with a system rigged against him. He is crying, I was crying, because he is slowing down on purpose to let the runner in second place catch him up, and he's doing it while ahead and on the home stretch with the crowd roaring, his fellow inmates cheering him on. He is crying because he knows losing will mean the loss of privileges he enjoyed while training, because he watched his father die, cancer, it's everywhere, but mainly because he is losing, because he can't not lose without losing his integrity, knowing that he deserves to win. So I was feeling the hopelessness but also the clarity of Colin's decision, grinding to a halt at centre stage, waiting for the runner, I mean actor, behind me to do his thing, when I thought I heard someone in the audience call me a dilettante in front of a thousand people.

'You're not doing it right,' the voice said, articulating my own thoughts and worries which I'd managed to put to one side while it'd all been happening fast.

'You're doing it wrong and you know it.' Gives me cold sweat thinking about it to this day.

'You what?' I said. I came out of character then.

'The intensity and also the content are offensive,' the voice said, bringing back the complainant from the sports shop, her lack of appreciation.

'Who said that,' I said, addressing the audience directly. 'Are you hearing this? Show yourself if you have something to say!'

'What's he talking about,' came a comment from a guy in the first row, combover, I can see him now. 'Who's he talking to?' 'He's not making any sense.' 'What's he doing with his arms.' 'He's holding his ears shut?' 'Somebody bring him a glass of water.'

I lost feeling in my hands and feet on account of over-breathing, I suspect. I folded forward, arms propped on my thighs, and just stood there, until someone, I couldn't say who, led me off stage. The surprise and indignation of the audience followed me into the depths of the backstage area and continues to follow me everywhere to this day, Korine. It is what it is. I mean, I wish it weren't but it is.

They didn't even give me a day before they removed me without explanation or follow-up. Replaced me with the understudy – RADA-educated, for what it's worth – for the remainder of the run. Can't remember his name, now that I think of it. There you go. Last lead in a major production I ever played. That was twenty-five years ago this March just gone. First step on the track that would land me, well, in the tracksuit.

Are you ever going to come out of the bathroom? Korine? What's he doing in there. Mind, I'd rather not know. Don't want to imagine.

If those early years taught me anything it was that I was an erratic actor. To do with that exact difference I'm trying to get at, that I carried around with myself and that shaped, fundamentally, how I went about acting. I had a style that was unfashionable and that, replicated by another actor, tended not to work. I tended to lay it on. Don't know why or how, but it worked when it worked. When it didn't, it really didn't. I'd deliver one night and the next, I wouldn't turn up, figuratively speaking. I didn't have the consistency that derives from professionalism and craft, whatever they teach you in drama school. Vital lessons I had missed. A related issue: acting, the way I went about it, the only way I knew how to, came at a cost. I tended to overapply myself to compensate for my perceived shortcomings. I'd put in the extra hours. Pull regular all-nighters. Consequently, I was on empty before even the pre-shows: please see, what happened that Tuesday night at the NT. No support from within the industry then, either. No awareness around mental health or social difference. Better now, I'm told. I doubt it.

Consistency is the death of good acting, I read that somewhere. May well be the case, but the lack of it would've been the death of me: after *The Loneliness of the Long Distance Runner*, I made a conscious effort to change tack. I'd met Laurie the year before, we were twenty-three twenty-four respectively. We had plans to move in together. Were committed to supporting each other. Maybe one day have a child. (We didn't.) I resolved to develop a pragmatism around acting. Treat acting like work. I'd go for supporting roles, anything that offered stability. I say this as if I had a choice: after what happened, the offers failed to materialise. I learnt that the industry is unforgiving, Korine.

In two-thousand-two, I landed the role which would define me, or fail to define me, as an actor for the subsequent two decades. Seventeen seasons, three hundred and eighty-four episodes, on *People Live, People Die, People Live as if They Were Already Dead*, the long-running series for the BBC and the international market. Ah! I knew that would get his attention. Yes, Korine, I did say *People Live, People Die, People Live as if They Were Already Dead*, you heard that correctly. Why does he sound so surprised, should I be offended. Yes, A. Smythe. And B. Smith, exactly. Revolved around the premise of one sleuth, A. Smythe, who was hired to keep watch on another sleuth, B. Smith, who was in turn hired to keep watch on A. Smythe. Unbeknownst to each other, neither Smythe nor Smith do anything other than observe each other, creating an existential feedback loop which the series exploited for tragicomic effect. I wasn't hired to play Smythe, nor Smith. I was hired to play Smythe's partner, C. Schmidt. For seventeen seasons, screen time of two to three minutes per half-hour episode, Schmidt attempted to get Smythe's attention unsuccessfully. Yes, him with the nose. A prosthetic, obviously. I hated it. Anyway, my counterpart, Smith's estranged wife, D. Smiff, was played by Drew Atkins, performing spectacularly within the limitations of her role, if I may say. In the beginning, I thought I had it made. This was the sort of part I'd been looking for: steady work. Cosy acting. Equity rates. Had I known then what I know now, I'd have never gone near it.

It started off well enough. In the early days, the writing was quick, the humour deadpan. The young director, Fran Howe – yes, her – valued resourcefulness on the part of the actors. There was room and even a need for improvisation to help accommodate an impossibly tight shooting schedule and shoestring budget. Halfway into a take, Howe might rotate her right wrist e.g., signalling to us actors to extend an underwritten scene or else to fast-forward a dirge. We liked it. Kept us on our toes. Mistakes were inevitable and went on to define the programme's aesthetic: shots showing microphone booms would appear in the final cut. Actors fluffing their lines, trying and failing to rescue the scene: all in there. Clapper loader walking into and out of a shot: say hello to the viewers at home. There was an audience for it. The programme acquired a following quickly.

After season two, Howe went on to better things, landing on *Terrace House* eventually, that's the twenty-eighteen BAFTA-winning ITV drama that made her. Her replacement, like her many subsequent replacements, preferred to stick to a script. It was the beginning of the end for *People*. I'm glad you agree, Korine. Jesus, the way he came out with it, is he a TV critic now. The series plateaued, and yet it kept running for another seventeen years. Me in it. My character Schmidt never evolved beyond his original constraints. I ran out of ways to fail to get a disinterested party's attention in circa two-thousand-four and so did the writers' room. Couldn't say how many times I said I would quit. Why don't you try for different parts, Laurie would say. What, and risk another *Long Distance Runner*, I didn't say. I'd lost it, you see. The feistiness at the heart of me: it was gone.

Inevitably, it came to a head. One day, September two-thousand-seventeen, I, alongside Drew Atkins and other supporting actors, was in make-up, four a.m. start. We were in the same studio in a business park outside Basildon, Essex, that we'd been shooting in for the last four or five years. Several dozens of noses, one per day plus spares, had been modelled from a cast custom-made for my face: a selection was lying there on a tray and tissue, like stillborn birds. Did I say, I as Schmidt wore a prosthetic nose. I did, did I. In the early years, I didn't think much of it. Later, I feared they were racialising the character through the back door. At one point, I mounted a one-man campaign to lose Schmidt's nose. No avail. The nose, I was told, was Schmidt's personality. I myself was more expendable than the nose. Had the advantage that I was rarely recognised in plain clothes, I tried taking comfort in that. Anyway, that morning, I was already in costume: an ill-fitting brown suit with light blue shirt, I'd developed an inflamed eyelid overnight on account of the copious amounts of make-up applied to blend silicone and skin the day before and the days before that and which had irritated the area. The MA wasn't the best I had, I will say. As soon as I sat in the make-up chair, Nancy P., with her purposeful wrist flicks on applying, her unsentimental way of pressing the back of a spoon, yes, against the puffy parts of my eyes, which were all of them, and my eyebrows, was making noises, blaming me for ruining what was meant to be a blank canvas: my face. 'Aubrey,' she sighed, injured party. 'What are you doing to me.' Then went to work straight away. The fact that the eyelid was red and swollen, swelling still, meant more make-up in Nancy's world.

I looked at Atkins – aka D. Smiff – for moral support. She sat in the chair next to me, sipping from a bottle of water. She raised her shoulders and arms, what can you do. If you weren't in low-level pain on the job, you weren't doing it right.

The assistant director checked in: 'Alright, all

good? Packed day today. Aubrey, what's with your eye. Nancy, what's with his eye. Why is his make-up running. Nance, can you touch him up? What scenes are you in today?' He was flicking through his multi-page shooting schedule.

I was meant to chase Smith through the car park outside, mistaking him for my character's partner, Smythe, as I had done once in two-thousand-two, and again in two-thousand-seven and -nine. I said something to that effect. The AD walked out of the room halfway through my reply, having spotted a technician he needed a word with in the corridor. Meanwhile, my eye started tearing under Nancy's renewed assault. An inconvenience for her and she let me know.

'Huw. Huwie!' The MA called over the runner. He looked about twelve. 'Get Clyde. Yes the director, is there another Clyde. I didn't think so.'

Five minutes later Huw returned with the director in tow. 'Make it quick, Nance. What is it.' Clyde: rude Scottish man, thirty-eight, thirty-nine. Moustache. Belt, shirt tucked in. 'Drew. Love. Looking good.' Atkins giving a sailor's salute. 'What's the problem then. Talk to me,' Clyde said.

'His eye,' Nancy said.

Clyde bent down, coming close to my face. He took his glasses off to see better. 'I know what you mean.'

'The concealer is running. The adhesive won't hold.' The MA pulled off my nose which had been hanging on by a thread. 'He flinches when I go near him.'

'Get rid of it, all of it, and start over.'

I must've audibly gulped: they turned to look at me as opposed to my eye and nose.

'Is that a problem, Aubrey? Huw, get me a paracetamol. No, two. Get me the whole pack. Now!'

Within minutes, the runner returned with a pack of painkillers.

'What, no water?' Clyde said. 'Huwie, think. How is he meant to get the tablets down without water. We pay you to participate intellectually, Huw. To apply common sense.'

He was here on a work placement and 'we' weren't paying him anything, Huw replied.

'Forget it,' I said. 'I'll get them down without water.' One, two. The uncoated variety. You know the feeling you get as if something is stuck in your throat but it actually isn't? There's a name for it? That. I coughed. Coughed again. Both eyes watering now. Streaming, actually.

'Jesus Christ, Aubrey.'

Atkins got up and handed me her bottle. I looked at her: thank you. What would I do without you.

'Give him five minutes,' the director said to the MA. 'More concealer. More glue. Make it work. You got this, Aub, yes? Yes?' He walked away talking into his headset. 'Can we get away without close-up? I didn't think so. Yeah, it'll be fine. They'll make it work. He in anything tomorrow? He is. How many scenes? Hm. In theory, could we get a replacement at short notice? Yes? Who. Huw who? Oh, Huwie. No, I like it. Let's run with it. Nance! Nancy! The nose goes on Huwie tomorrow. The runner, that's right. He'll be fine. Not a lot of acting to Schmidt, is there. It's all in the nose.'

I'd rather stack shelves at Tesco than keep doing this, I said to Laurie that night. We lived on the Golden Lane Estate then, round the corner from here, Stanley Cohen House. Let's just wait, Laurie said. Not the time to make major life changes. She'd developed a sore throat that wouldn't go. She'd been having difficulties swallowing. So she'd seen the GP. Had been referred to the hospital. Had waited six weeks for the scan, another two for the biopsy. We were currently one week into the wait for the results. I made a tactless joke about a paracetamol tablet stuck in her throat. I have to live with that now. Eventually, Laurie received her diagnosis.

The subsequent four years just happened. I continued on *People* and Laurie, an academic, a cultural theorist, continued to work until she no longer could. Less than half a year after her death they cancelled the programme. Not a minute too soon, did he just say that. Very funny, Korine. Very funny. How's the bathroom treating you by the way? At your own pace: just thought I'd check. On top of losing my wife, Korine, I lost my source of income, so I moved from Stanley Cohen House into the Aldersgate sublet to make our savings last longer: one of the reasons anyway. I stepped into my tracksuit. Called it a day. Now you know: the extent of my problem. I'm going to have to have a look, aren't I. I know he is in there: the bathroom door isn't shut. I can hear movement. Fidgeting. Korine? Knock knock. You still there? Course you are. He's folded down the toilet seat, is sitting on it. Hands in his lap, legs crossed awkwardly. Looking at me.

Anyway, last week, Howe got in touch via my (former) agent. Original *People* director, a lot of mutual respect between us. In a sense, I blame Howe for you, Korine. Don't take it personally. God, so sensitive. At my request, we met at the Barbican lake. This was yesterday.

'Good to see you,' Howe said. 'God you got old.'

She hadn't. She was wearing aviator glasses, strong prescription, and grey jogging bottoms. Her sweatshirt saying *Terrace House* in a stylised font. She didn't know how much my agent had told me, she said. She was looking to cast the lead in *As If*, an eight-part adaptation of an overlooked novel: an unofficial – that is, uncredited – spin-off of *People*, as it were. The book centred a C. Schmidt derivative character, in this instance called Cyril. 'That's Schmidt getting what he deserves, Lewis. What do you think.'

My wife died from cancer of the throat, I thought. It came and went, came back, went again, and then, it went everywhere.

Howe could've got anyone for the part, but she wanted me. She knew what I could do with the character, given the chance. I knew it, too. Let's make him what he should've been in the first place. History correcting itself, for once.

I quit acting, I said. Hadn't she heard.

'Aubrey, please. The role has your name on it. You owe it to yourself. To your audience. To Laurie!'

'Thanks, but no thanks. I couldn't if I wanted to.' Look at me: I indicated my tracksuit, my Oxfords, my various vulnerabilities: none of it put her off.

'Think about it. Take the novel at least. See for yourself.'

I got up to leave. What was there to think about. I'd been thinking about nothing but for almost forty years. What good did it do. I accepted the paperback, azure blue and light brown, black typeface, to be polite.

Next thing I know, I'm seeing you, Lindsey Korine. That's less than twenty-four hours later. Consider the causal immediacy: stressful event, you: QED. In that sense, Korine, you are the problem. Since you asked.

3

Who is he. By which I mean, what happened to him. What did he say his name was, Lewis. Aubrey Lewis. Two syllables twice, like Lindsey Korine. He looks like death warmed up, I mean, death: too cold for warm anything. Is he depressed? I'd be if I lived here. This chair is killing me, by the way. Unsupportive of the human form in every way. Huh! I gave myself a fright then. Thought someone was coming at me from behind. Looming in the corner, a secret third person: he's-behind-you standard scenario. But it's just a coat stand. Oh: a coat stand. Worth exploring. Worth having a closer look. Now we're getting somewhere. Old outerwear, worse for wear on first sight. But if you appreciate quality. If you know what to look for. Whoever bought these, once, had money. Do actors have money? Lewis is an actor, he just said that. Sorry: *was* an actor. Personally, I don't see it.

I don't see him on TV, I mean, in my mind's eye. Not terrible looking, if you like that sort of thing. Striking face. Tall. But the state of him. I've rarely seen worse and I've seen bad. Think contents of a Hampstead charity shop, that's the coats again. No. No. Maybe. No. Let's try this one. Too small. Christ, way too small. It's my height: I don't have to try very hard to lay my hand flat on the ceiling e.g. High, by the way. Corniced. Woodchip wallpaper, bubbling in places on account of historical water ingress. Flat hasn't been decorated for decades. Old London. Clerkenwell, to be precise: still around, in the face of it. The Barbican Estate across the road, visible through the front-facing window. Golden Lane Estate to the left. Can't see my building, can I? No. I could have been a fashion model on account of my height. Was approached by a scout once in the early nineties, was it. Told her where to go: was what we were like then. Incorrigible. Not easily taken in. Do I regret it? Can't say I do! No regrets has been my MO, or my motto, which is it, for the longest time. No point wishing I could do the past differently. Anyway, I've managed: the boxy tweed coat and the wax jacket, one on top of the other. Fancy that: a wax jacket. Never wore one in my life. A country thing, I believe. Countrycore.

Warmer already. Is there a mirror? No mirror, at least not in the living room. And what's with the boxes everywhere. Why has he not unpacked. Can't do it, poor love. I ask again: what happened to him. Put me away if I'm ever as depressed as he looks. Am I depressed? After what I did? If anything, I'm up. I'm a hundred miles an hour. If there's any part of me that's depressed, it's this place doing it. But what's this. Cute! Cutie! An angel, is it? Let's get you on display. I like Christmas. What's not to like, I don't get it. My child likes it. I like it because of my child. What now, Lewis giving himself a panic attack. 'You're over-breathing, love. Yes. You know how to regulate your breathing?' He's doing it. Good. He keeps doing this thing with his eyes, opening and closing them in quick succession, and saying little things to himself. Words to live by, I trust, for his sake. I'll leave it with the decor for now. Preferable not to fall out with my host. I'll lie low, literally, here on the sofa. Here we go. Easier said than done: it's too short. Who designs these things. For who. What if I turned on my back: edge of it in the bend of my knees now, no thanks. We're not doing that. Let me sit up again. Better. What is he doing. He just excused himself and walked out of the room. That's the tap going in the bathroom I suspect, I have yet to get the tour of the flat. His wife died, did he just say that. I'm sorry. I really am. Young as well. Mid-forties, I'd say. No age. My age. My wife's age. That would explain the state he's in. That would do it. Aaand: we're back. Lewis standing in the middle of the room like he's seeing a ghost. How is he surprised to see me. I've been here for a while now. We've been getting to know each other. I mean, Lewis, it's me, Korine! He doesn't want me to leave, does he? Why! So he can get back to not reading whatever book he's not reading? Now *I'm* getting stressed. He wouldn't throw me out, would he. He has a kind face. I think. What does that even mean, a kind face: faces are versatile. Faces have range, hence the capacity to be anything but kind. Not that he actually asked me to leave. Unless this is him asking in not as many words: blinking and talking to himself. Walking in and out of the room for no apparent reason. But I'm not here to interpret physical theatre: if he wants me gone, he'll have to say so outright. Thing is, I couldn't leave if he asked me to. I have nowhere to go. Laurie saying if I walk out now, I won't be coming back that's for sure. She meant it, too. That was two days ago, give or take. Feels a lot longer: wandering the streets with no aim disrupts one's appreciation of time's passage, as it turns out.

'Is there a problem?' I didn't just say that. What if he says yes: I'm literally prompting him. Playing into his hands. I'm minded to take a step back before I say anything else stupid. Give him a moment to get himself together as well. We don't have to fall out, Lewis, do we. No good for either of us. Is there a problem, Jesus Christ. I'm my own worst enemy sometimes.

I can confirm: the radiator in the bathroom is also inoperative. Who cares anymore: I'm toasty as is. The difference a decent coat makes. Coats, plural. Lewis talking in the other room, I can half hear him. A lot to say, all of a sudden. As if someone turned on the tap. I'll allow it. If it helps calm him down. Well, hello. That's me in the mirrored cabinet now. I've seen worse, I must say. I wonder if I should clip back my fringe like Lewis. Emphasise my eyelashes. They are long. *Long* long. Dare I say, longer than Lewis's. I could have been an actor. Wouldn't want to. You'd have to be driven to do it, especially if you're from the sort of background that I'm from. A lot of toiling for scant reward, I expect. Never any guarantees, I mean, listen to him. Life story, are we doing this now.

I myself remember wanting to be an actor for about a minute age ten or eleven, having seen Gary Oldman in *Prick Up Your Ears* on TV. The title a play on prick up your arse, I got that at eleven. The exact sort of joke I was well versed in. That went round the playground, of my school anyway. I remember my mum confiscating the remote and switching the telly off halfway through. Deemed the content unsuitable. Not that she was overly prim when it came to the sorts of programmes she liked. Anyway, Oldman was spellbinding in it. Went to our secondary school twenty years ago. Not that you'd know it, they never made much of him being an alumnus. Missed opportunity, if you ask me. They wouldn't have fooled us anyway: we all knew Oldman made it despite his schooling, not because of it. If anyone even thought of having a go at acting at my school, they knew better than to seriously pursue it. A fool's errand, despite Oldman's one-in-a-million example, or even because of it: if he made it, the chances of another one making it had to be close to zero. Not sure that's correct. Probability calculus, not my strong suit. It might have been had I put my mind to it. I never put my mind to pretty much anything. None of us did. Trying per se was frowned upon, and for good reason: you'd set yourself up for failure. You're forever up against it and then, when it all goes wrong, inevitably, you end up worse than to start off with. Lewis confirms it: listen to him. Should never have bothered. Commonsensical not to participate in a losing game.

Something coming back to me now. Haven't thought about it, him, in years: kid in my class, always on his own in the remote part of the schoolyard. Always talking to himself. Certainly had a lot to say considering no one was listening. He tended to hold the top of his hair up with an elastic hair tie, bright turquoise, the kind girls wore round their wrists at the time: bold. Too bold for his own sake, arguably. The day I went up to him and asked what he was doing. How about he came and played football with us instead of talking to the fence. We were kicking a ball over there. He couldn't, he said. He was rehearsing a monologue from – whatever – it meant nothing to me. Did I want to hear a bit. Er, no. Was I sure? I was sure. Suit yourself, I said finally and rejoined the kickabout. What was I doing, talking to that fool, Harvey Kemp the team captain said. Was I queer. I must be queer, like my boyfriend over there. I laughed it off, but the comment, and the sight of him with the hair tie doing his thing in the face of it all, neither would leave me for a while. Kemp was right, the kid was a fool, and yet, I admired him almost in spite of myself: he was more himself than I'd ever be, I knew it instinctively.

Come again? *The Loneliness of the Long Distance Runner*? I read that. I'm a reader, always have been. Novels, plays, pretty indiscriminately. Tends to surprise people. If he mops your floor, if he drives your minicab, if he works in data entry, he doesn't read, is the general assumption. Suits me. I appreciate the relative invisibility I suppose. Comes with its own sort of power-from-below, or so I'm told. Strength in blending in, not standing out. God, he can talk. Spilling now. He's been on his own for too long, is what it is. It's doing him good, too: he seems less hostile, for starters. As if he wants me to hear him. Act as a witness, maybe. What's this: *People Live, People Die, People Live as if They Were Already Dead*? He didn't. He did not just say that. I used to watch that. It isn't still going, is it? Please tell me it isn't still going. I watched that religiously, strange expression, when I worked as a security guard at that place on Finsbury Square: a media company, if I remember correctly. Early two-thousands, was it. Lots of monitors showing CCTV footage and a cheeky one showing *People*, BBC Two, one to one thirty a.m. graveyard slot. Me, feet on the desk, Edam sandwich in hand, no complaints. Who was he in it. I have to tell Laurie. Laurie likes *People* as much as the next pers— Schmidt? I don't believe it. He seems different in real life. He must be a decent actor to seem so different in real life. As if his very facial features adapted to the role, how is this possible. Wouldn't have recognised him in a million years, is what I'm trying to say.

Lewis standing in the door frame now. Don't mind me, love. I'll sit quietly on the lid of your toilet for as long as it takes. Wouldn't want to interrupt your confession. Schmidt, I see it now. In fact, I can't unsee it.

'I got offered the role,' Lewis says.

What role.

The lead role in a major BBC production, apparently. A novel adaptation connected to *People*: a re-evaluation of the Schmidt character, newly named Cyril. Exclusive audition with the producer and casting director a mere formality, he was told. Tomorrow, as it were: not going to happen. He isn't up to it. He declined.

I see. After everything he just told me, he isn't

going to audition. It's not like he's overextended exactly. Why pass up a rare opportunity. Help me make sense of it. Not a thought to the fact that he owes it to himself to try. Owes it, frankly, to the rest of us.

I'll explain. Let me explain: when I said I couldn't see it? Him on TV? I wasn't entirely honest with myself. When earlier tonight I was sitting in the Barbican underpass, Beech Street I think the official name is, I must've seen something. I was sitting on the pavement, leaning against one of the panels cladding the walls: a chipper palette of beige and its foils: light blue, maroon, white, bright yellow, I want to say sand. I considered my options: walking into the oncoming traffic was one of them. I'm sorry, it was. Sitting there, the other. I think I was hugging my legs. I can turn this around, I kept telling myself. I might not see how, but I can turn this around. Which was when Lewis, didn't know him as Lewis then, passed on the other side in his cream-coloured tracksuit. Strange how he blended in with his environment, I thought, but acted as a beacon at the same time: someone explain that to me. He headed towards the Aldersgate Street exit. I didn't know why I followed him, but I can speculate: for starters, he didn't not look like me. Tall but not as tall, the discrepancy could be postural. He was paler. His eyes puffier. If likes do in fact attract likes it would've explained it. Or perhaps Lewis was wearing the sort of track top I would've given my left arm for at that point: I was perishing in the cold. Clever way he wore it, tucked in like that, it made an impression. In the state I was in, I would've followed the track top, its wearer, to the ends of the earth. Or it could've been that Beech Street had exhausted its hospitality. That Lewis was the first person who'd walked past at the precise moment when I needed, desperately, to move on. Get myself out of the underpass on account of the exhaust fumes, for one thing: they exacerbated my asthma. In all likelihood, I would've gone after anyone I caught sight of. I might have registered Lewis's vulnerability and decided to exploit it. Or else, I registered his vulnerability and decided that this person, this walking SOS, needed my help. On a subconscious level, I might have recognised Schmidt, marginal character in a television series long past its sell-by date, or maybe just maybe I recognised the strange kid from school: elastic hair tie, bright turquoise, replaced by a tight row of kirby grips. If I didn't, if it wasn't any of these things that led me to follow him, I'm now thinking that I picked up on this actor thing I'm trying to get at. Some sort of stage presence – off-stage presence, even – that made him stand out. Point being, he has a responsibility to put that to use. To use it to pull himself out of this hole he's fallen into. If Aubrey Lewis can't save himself, what hope is there for anyone else.

What do you mean, you don't want to talk about it. Didn't seem like it this last hour or so. Fine, whatever. You go to bed. Sleep on it. See how you feel in the morning. Don't mind me. Leave the door ajar, if only for my sake. I'll sit in the living room, wide awake. No rest for the wicked. A biblical phrase, doesn't make it any less true. Most of the rest of it I can't get behind. Can't abide it actually. Sweet dreams to you, too. And he's off. Seriously.

He's not blaming me, is he? Lewis seems to blame me for the fact that he can't or won't attend his audition tomorrow. As if I were the final nail in his coffin and a sign, if one were needed, that he isn't well. I won't take it on. I feel guilty enough as it is. He's having a personality crisis, is what it is. A crisis of confidence. He needs to remember who he is, for Christ's sake. She's been dead, how long? Needs to stop feeling sorry for himself and get back on that horse. Not how it works, I gather. Seven stages, more like seven million. Didn't kick me out, though, did he. There's that to be grateful for.

What's in here then, cardboard box number two. More Christmas cheer? No. Newspaper clippings. Flyers, going way back. Schmidt autograph cards, why's that so funny to me! An oversize sheet of paper folded into small squares, ok let's see you. Wow, it's enormous. Two metres and a half by two metres, if I had to guess. Look at that: *The Loneliness of the Long Distance Runner* at the National Theatre, nineteen-ninety-nine, Lewis at the centre of it. How young he was. Confrontational attitude. Eyelashes to die for, and those shorts he's wearing, they put him in those deliberately. What must his mother have thought when these went up all over town. The bus stops along the Old Kent Road, you used to see that sort of thing there. Did *I* see it at the time? The poster, not the play. Not on my radar, really. Prohibitive ticket prices, too. Anyway, it's decided: this is going up. Here on the big wall facing the door. Aspirational. Or inspirational, is it. Most importantly: motivational. Should give him the push he needs to get him to the audition in the morning. Remind him of his glory days. Now where does he keep his sellotape. Or blu-tack. Blu-tack will do. First drawer I look in, there it is. How did I do that! It's meant to be. Right upper corner, then left. God, it's large. Here, here and here, and another bit here for good measure. And it's up: Aubrey Lewis, larger-than-life-size, defying the limitations of his own social background. Makes me question whether it was just my dad who made himself invisible and called it a virtue. Whether it was just Harvey Kemp, the school bully, who called difference queer. Did I pick up their bollocks and live by it: something to contemplate. I'm starting to sound like Laurie. Best not to dwell on it. I'll end up overthinking. What next. I should put the latch on the front door, for starters. Anyone free to walk in.

4

It starts to rain as soon as I step out the front door. What did I expect. This is England, it rains. This is me, Lindsey Korine, en route to the National Theatre Rehearsal Studio for eleven a.m., on Lewis's behalf. It gives me no pleasure to say, I'll audition in his stead. Because he can't or he won't. Bystanding isn't an option: not in the context of my own wide-ranging disaster. Speaking of which – no. Not now. I have enough problems as it is: I left the wax jacket at home on account of its smell. What was I thinking. Now the woollen coat is getting wet, developing its own animal odour. I picture myself walking into the rehearsal room to meet the director, calling to mind a slaughter-bound lamb, literally. What will she be like, the director. Howe, is it? Fran Howe. She? Or he? She'll take me for Lewis, of course. Hard not to. We do look alike, I will say the resemblance is curious.

Which will work in my favour. The director is already invested in Lewis. She'll want him, me, to do well. Question is, who else will be in the room. Who else will I need to impress. Am I mad for thinking I can do this. I must be mad. What am I doing. Help.

Suffice to say, the poster did not have the effect I hoped it would. It didn't just not motivate: he didn't like it. That's how I interpreted his no-no-no-no-ing anyway. He kept saying no, looking at it. Looking away. Looking back at it. Then he laughed. It wasn't a happy laugh. Was it? I don't know him well enough yet to be certain. Anything could mean anything really. A whole spectrum of feelings in his face at any one time. I came down on the side of no, not happy, the laughter was deranged. The kind that makes people nervous. I almost wished I hadn't put up the poster in the first place. What can I say, I meant well. No regrets, oh stop it, I'm annoying myself. Into Farringdon Street now, is that right? The area has changed beyond recognition this last decade. Old people say that. Am I old people, I must be. I don't feel it. I feel it. Both. Half an hour's walk to Waterloo tops. If I step lively. Disregard the pain in my side. When the laughter stopped, Lewis sat down on the reddish-black chair he dislikes, put his head in his hands and ignored me. That was new. I believe that at some point during the night or early morning he arrived at the decision to ignore me completely. Refusing to look me in the eye when I parked myself directly in front of him was him living by his decision. Hard not to take it personally. I try not to. Then he started trembling, just subtly, I barely noticed at first. I asked if he was cold and should we request for the communal heating to be turned back on. He didn't answer. He got up abruptly, picked up his phone and keys from the windowsill and left the flat.

Where did he go, he didn't say. There is a small chance he's planning to audition without telling me. If so, good. If I see him en route, I'll make sure he goes in, then hang back and wait outside the building. Or I might slip in behind him and try to watch. But what if he isn't. What if he's putting distance between himself and the National Theatre Rehearsal Studio as we speak. What if, at eleven a.m., he's nowhere near where he's expected to be. In that case, I will be. Good lord, have I thought this through. Across Blackfriars Bridge now: the short stretch of the way that is covered, at last. The river is high and brown and yet sparkling, how does that work. I'm wearing a pair of cotton trousers of much the same colour: pleated, held up with a belt. It was the closest I felt I was able to get to 'European cultured' with what was available in Lewis's flat. Good to get out of the pyjama bottoms, I must say: they outstayed their welcome. I exchanged my sliders for a pair of Puma Oslos, the only pair of shoes I found that fit. They are wrong: notably unworn old-man trainers. Hard and bright. Nothing I can do about it. Anyway, fringe pinned back and to the side Lewis-style, to work the illusion. I've been wearing it like this anyway since last night. Looks good, in my opinion. It suits me. What if Howe knows I'm not him. We might look alike, but unlike Lewis, I'm not an actor: Howe and the industry professionals will be able to tell? Out of the two of us, I am the one with a modicum of preparation, I have that on my side. I don't just mean that I'm dressed the part, the clothes are a mere expression of my hard-won preparedness. Let me rewind a bit: after I put up the poster, I went back to unpacking. Might as well give the sad man a hand, I thought, whether he likes it or not. In the process, I found several textbooks on acting. I was intrigued so I stopped what I was doing and read two or three, cover to cover. Fascinating stuff and, coincidentally, containing a ton of advice I thought might help put him in the right frame of mind for the audition. Jump-start his actor self, so to speak. I imagined us going through some of the exercises I bookmarked, by way of top-corner folds, including the repetition exercise and the *yes, and* improvisation warm-up. I will say I proceeded to go down a series of rabbit holes, watching acting videos on his laptop. (Password on a Post-it note on the wall, not a problem.) There was one, shot across several very similar acting classes in the seventies eighties, in a drama school in Brooklyn, New York. To the left of the room, by a row of high windows, Sandy M., one of the most influential and revered acting teachers in modern times, sits behind a desk. Two acting students, white, one female one male, are standing in front of him. Facing them, an audience of circa fifteen students on chairs. As a result of throat cancer – it is everywhere – Sandy uses oesophageal speech, inhaling and manipulating air in the oesophagus to create vocal sounds in the absence of a voice box, in combination with a microphone attached to the black plastic frames of his glasses. Gives his voice a mechanical and may I say superhuman sound, incidentally. He instructs the students to concentrate on their partner and repeat exactly what they do until they sense a minuscule shift in behaviour or affect, which in turn prompts a response in them. They are then to follow their instinct and move the interaction beyond direct repetition. Sandy observes, wheezes sporadically, interrupts as necessary, which is often. Watching the clip, I couldn't tell whether or not the students were doing it right. Somewhat disturbingly, neither could they. (They were not.) What I, we, were acutely aware of were Sandy's reactions, including holding his head in his hands at one point, despairing at the students' incompetence and lack of talent. Takeaway for me: there is more to acting than just pretending to be somebody else. Chances are, you aren't doing it right, without even knowing. In hindsight, I wish I didn't see the video. Don't need it in my head, to be honest. At half-four a.m., I tried to get Lewis out of bed. He waved my hand away where I shook his shoulder but didn't wake up. Maybe he'd taken something. Fair enough. I went back into the living room. Because it was there, I had a go at the novel, *As If*, a particular chapter of which I knew had been chosen for him to perform at the audition. It was very interesting. The idea is for Cyril to pursue Darryl (the restyled – 'decolonised', he'd said – version of *People*'s D. Smiff) on the behest of Beryl (formerly B. Smith). At the same time, Errol (A. Smythe) hires Darryl to pursue Cyril. In other words, the premise of *As If* is identical to the premise of *People*, but, in a the-last-shall-be-the-first-the-first-last sort of biblical or Fanonian inversion, the original supporting cast is elevated to leads and vice versa, and the genre is realism-by-default in keeping with the literary zeitgeist. Where is it by the way. I mean, the book. Here, in my coat pocket. I need it. It contains notes I made on emphasis, pronunciation, shifts in sentiment and so on. South of the river now. Have they redirected the traffic again: completely disorientating. I better concentrate or I'll end up in Vauxhall. By the time Lewis finally woke up, eight a.m., I could recite parts of his audition piece. I was still thinking I was doing this to help him prepare, that I'd go through the text with him, quickly, then send him off. Godspeed! Break a leg! It wasn't until he broke down in his chair after seeing the poster, holding his head in his hands, covering his ears and shutting me out, that the thought came to me: I could do it for him. I might have to, if I wanted it done. Waterloo station, old heap, looking grey on a rainy day. You've seen better days, too. Not since I've been around, mind. What now, left into The

Cut. There it is already, at the corner: the National Theatre Rehearsal Studio. Jesus Christ. I am buying him time, is all there is to it. With a bit of luck, I'll get through the audition, keep the process alive. Give Lewis a chance to come to his senses. I'll know that I did that for him, I'll always have that. Something to be proud of at last.

I'm inside the building. Glass and concrete, very airy. The word pristine springs to mind. Whereas I'm dripping, I am a contaminant. I'm also late. First scan of the foyer confirms that Lewis isn't here. Onwards then. Rehearsal room two-oh-four, I biroed it on my hand. Thank god I had the foresight: my head has retained nothing. Must be two floors up. I'm nervous now, why. What can go wrong. The inability to envisage worse is a limitation of the imagination, I read that somewhere. Or was it the inability to envisage better? Doesn't matter. Why am I out of breath going up two flights of stairs, is a whole other question. I'm here, at last. The door is ajar: in I go. Bloody hell, the room is enormous. Floor-to-ceiling windows. Parquet flooring and more naked concrete (the walls). They don't expect me to fill this space with my presence never mind voice, do they. Strikes me that being tall won't do it. Don't swallow, Korine, gives your fear away. Do not swallow. 'Ah!' I wave. Must be Howe at the far end of the room, by the longish table. I like her glasses. She comes towards me. Big smile. Hug coming in. Says 'how tall you are' in a strange Little Red Riding Hood what-big-teeth-you-have register. She's not on to me, is she? I make myself smaller, closer to Lewis's height. Sinking in on myself. We come out of the embrace. Howe's sweatshirt is wet because of me. I apologise profusely. 'Aubrey,' Howe says, leading me to the table. Two currently unoccupied chairs behind it are facing a lonely chair: mine. 'Meet Mehmet Farouqi and—' I can't quite hear the other guy's name, Kelsey or Kelly Hughes. Rain prattling against the expanse of glass facing The Cut, that's why. Farouqi is the assistant director, the AD, I'm told, Hughes the BBC producer. I notice a small camera on a tripod facing the lonely chair. In a matter of minutes, I will sit on the latter and deliver the scene I've prepared. I will be fine. I went over it must've been hundreds of times. Acted it out, with mirror, without.

'Shall we?' the AD says.

Howe gives me a conspiratorial smile, as if to say impress them, Lewis. I know you will.

'You want me here? On this chair?' I'm stating the obvious. Stalling.

Howe and Hughes sit down on the chairs behind the table. Farouqi positions himself behind the digicam, looking through the viewfinder on top. Three sets of eyes on me, I feel exposed. I'm still upright next to the chair, it feels dangerous to sit down. The room just went dark on account of the worsening weather. Howe asks the AD if he could switch the big light on please. He walks all the way across the room. The clacks of his heels on parquet like a firing squad having a field day, me against the wall obviously. The ceiling lights come on and I actually flinch. I sit down. We wait until Farouqi is back in situ. He manipulates the camera, zooming in and out, I imagine. In, more likely. On me.

'Whenever you're ready,' Howe says.

Suddenly, this person walks through the door. At first, I'm grateful for the disruption. Tall guy, my age, walking up to us in big, confident strides. His clothes are bone dry. He isn't sweating. Came in a cab, I conclude. It's Lewis, I think as he comes nearer. Christ almighty, it's Lewis, turning up to the audition even later than myself. He will lose his shit, seeing me here. Howe will lose her shit. Hughes will, too. I have no right, no business, who do I think I am. I half get up from the chair. I'm ready to run. The person I have down as Lewis approaches. No more than twelve metres, ten metres away now. He has his eyes trained on Howe. He is wearing a jacket that might count as a track top, in a pale brown which in a certain light might be perceived as beige. Actually, it is some sort of blazer. He isn't Lewis. Not anywhere near. I sit back down. Melt where I sit et cetera.

'Rehearsal room two-oh-four?' the man who isn't Lewis says in an RP accent. His fringe isn't clipped to the side. Something silvery is catching the light in the vicinity of his right ear, it seems like. An earring: is it called a hoop? If it's tiny?

'Lucien Jelley,' Hughes says, side-eyeing me. 'You're early.'

'Am I?'

'Would you mind waiting outside.'

'The corridor?'

'If you don't mind.'

He does mind, but goes off to wait outside. I look at Howe who looks to the floor. Who is this guy? Another actor invited to read for the role? I was under the impression this was an exclusive audition: should I say something? I can't think what role other than the lead Jelley would be considered for in *As If*. Smythe, perhaps, or Smith. Unless he is lined up for the position as my, Lewis's, understudy. Do they employ understudies in TV? Or is that the theatre. A stunt double? Or is he the second choice, some sort of back-up? Again, I try to read Howe's demeanour. Inscrutable, to me anyway.

'Where were we,' Hughes says. Can't tell if he's embarrassed or not.

Howe, simultaneously: 'I'm sorry about that.'

I fish the paperback out of my coat pocket. It got a bit wet. I apologise. Why. Why would they care. I take off my coat. Hang it over the back of the chair. I force myself not to apologise again; to repress the need to apologise constantly. I try to open the paperback on the relevant page, supposedly bookmarked. Looks like the folded top corner came unfolded in my pocket. I leaf through the pages trying to locate the passage in question. Where is it.

Farouqi looks up from behind the camera.

'One moment. I'm sor— sorry.' I apologise for almost apologising.

'Take your time,' the AD says, meaning I don't have all day.

There. Ok. I cross my legs. I uncross my legs. I read the first couple of words of my monologue. It comes out too quietly. Howe and Hughes are leaning forward to hear, I can see it from the corner of my eye. I stop to start over. 'Sorry, I'll go again.' I clear my throat. Same two lines, booming now. Hughes startles, I saw that, too: I am hyperaware of my surroundings. This time I push on, regulating the volume as I go. I'm completely disconnected from what I'm reading. I'm the opposite of disappearing into my act. According to one of the textbooks I studied, I'm meant to disappear into whatever action I'm performing. Maybe the fact that I don't doesn't show? I'm doing ok and don't know it? Unless I'm doing worse than I think I'm doing. I'm reminded of the time when someone, a teacher or parent, placed me, aged six, at the top of an indoor ski slope decorated with red and blue gates that did not, however, translate into a slalom course in my head. When the starting pistol went, I hurtled down the slope in a straight line: promptly disqualified. Reading, I'm trying not to fall over the words, which however I do, repeatedly. Words I never fell over when practising, not once. Words I didn't know had trip-up potential. Besides, I have developed a strange lisp, or I am noticing for the first time that I have a strange, almost revolting way of pushing air through my front teeth while enunciating. I fear I'm pulling faces.

No faces: worst thing you can do, according to one YouTube video, is grimacing. Scale it down. *Down*. When you're in close-up, you're meant to do basically nothing, such is the subtlety required when acting for camera. Unless I am acting for a live audience in this instance: Howe, Hughes, Farouqi, do they constitute a live audience? While still debating in my head, live audience or camera, I find that I've frozen. I'm doing nothing to the extent that my face is completely immobile. Despite the kirby grips, sweat is dripping into my eyes. The letters I'm trying to read are blurring, I lose my place on the page. And yet I push on. I'm not making much sense, I can tell. First sense of shame now, presenting itself as the impulse to stop, get up and walk out the door, or stay seated, melt and drip onto the parquet floor.

'Can I stop you there,' Howe says. 'Can I ask. How do you see him. What does he want.'

'Who?' I ask, knowing full well who.

'The character. Cyril.'

I let the paperback fall on my higher knee. I know it inside out and yet I draw a blank: what *is* Cyril about. 'I'm sorry,' I say, tenth or eleventh time over the course of the audition. I am so confused I don't know who I am anymore. Not Lewis, that has become clear. I'm not Lewis and never will be. 'I'm sorry for wasting your time.' I get up and pick up my coat. 'Aubrey,' Howe says. I can't look at her. I'll spare her the embarrassment of talking to me and make for the door. I feel eyes on my back. I forget how to put one foot in front of the other. I'm doing something self-conscious with my hips, too, I can tell. Door. There is the door. Not far now.

In the corridor, I see Jelley, the second choice, sitting on the floor. I notice his loafers. White socks. He is leaning against the wood-panelled wall, doing vocal exercises. Some strange sort of humming, an ascending scale: sounds like ridicule to my ears. I walk past without as much as acknowledging him.

Outside, it's stopped raining. I feel better in the fresh air. What just happened and – I instantly go there – can I fix it? What if I went back in and apologised *again*. Explained I was having an off day. I'm ill. Atmospheric pressure is affecting my BP. My, Lewis's, wife died. Considering whatever catastrophe of not my own making happened to me, could I please get a second chance? I could ask to reschedule and persuade, really persuade, Lewis to go. Or I could come clean: I could walk back in there and tell Howe in no uncertain terms that I am not him.

I meant well. Underestimated the task at hand. No point punishing Lewis for my mistake. That car wasn't going to stop, was it. 'It's a zebra crossing!' Prick. I can't go back, can I. Not after this. I've blown it, is all there is to it: a humbling experience. But what if I say I prepared the wrong role. I read the wrong book entirely. This thing here? *As If*? First time I saw it, just now, at the audition! What was it doing there, in my pocket! Not bad, don't get me wrong. Just not what I was expecting. I prepared *King Lear*. *Teletubbies*. Yes. This could work. Sounds plausible, I mean, it does to me. Speaking of *As If*: where is my copy. I must've left it in there. Don't tell me I left it in the rehearsal room. What if they look inside and see my amateurish annotations. Is there no end to the humiliation? What if, back at the flat, Lewis learns that I lost his book and insists I replace it. How. With what.

'Aubrey!' Someone calling his name. I hope it isn't me doing it. Is it? No. My mouth isn't moving any more than during the worst parts of the audition.

'Aubrey, wait!'

Howe? It's Howe catching up with me. She is holding out Lewis's paperback copy of *As If*. It's in a pitiful state.

'You left this behind,' she says.

'I'm not Lewis,' I say at the same time.

'Come again?'

'I'm not Lewis,' I say again. I regret it immediately. I can't even keep *this* charade up. I'm a terrible actor. The worst.

'What do you mean.'

'I mean I invented this character, Lindsey Korine. He attends auditions for me.'

'I see,' Howe says, sliding the book into the pocket of my coat. 'Nice to meet you, "Lindsey".' She is playing along rather than taking me at face value. She heard, I assume, of the death of my, Lewis's, wife. Heard I'd turned funny-peculiar as a result and is prepared to overlook it.

'He's an amateur,' I say.

'Lindsey is?'

'He can't act.'

'He got you the role, you know.'

'He didn't.'

'He did.'

'I was good?'

Howe laughs. She wouldn't go that far. 'Aubrey, Lindsey, please hear this.' The BBC told her she could do what she wanted if she stayed under a four-mil budget for the series. Fringe benefit of a commercial hit (she is referring to *Terrace House*). This, *As If*, with me, Aubrey Lewis, is what she wants to do. 'I know what you're capable of,' she says. 'I've seen it.'

'And Hughes?'

'Let me deal with Hughes,' she says. 'Lindsey Korine, huh,' she adds after a pause.

'Present.'

'Can you pass on a message to Aubrey Lewis please: filming starts in early July. All-cast read-through confirmed for the twenty-eighth of June. Please attend, prepared and in person.'

'You'll know him by his tracksuit,' I say, madly, gratefully, making my little promises.

5

I did it, I thought as I headed back north over Waterloo Bridge. The role was officially Lewis's. Now, how to break the news. Chances were, he would take offence at the fact I'd auditioned in his place. Well, he'd thank me in the long run. What Laurie used to say: you'll thank me in the et cetera. Case of the result justifying the means. But what if he actually meant what he'd said: that he didn't want or feel able to take on a major role at all. Either way, he would take some convincing. It would be critical to communicate gently. He wouldn't have to be on his own with it, I would say. I would help. I was in between jobs, as it were. As luck would have it. During the weeks leading up to the read-through – and for the length of the subsequent shoot if he'd have me – I would be his live-in scene partner, acting coach, confidant. In return, I'd exist in proximity to rare talent, I wouldn't say. Wouldn't want to sound sycophantic. He probably got that a lot. But privately, I knew exactly what was in it for me: I'd witness someone, Lewis, pull himself back from the brink and derive hope from it for myself. Besides, I might learn something. Free lodgings: that, too. That, above all. I would mention the shooting schedule, I would have to. Yes, it was soon. A lot of momentum behind the production: a positive. Enormous amount of work to do in a relatively short period of time? Not a problem: I was here to help. Yes.

When I returned to the flat, Lewis wasn't back. I had a bad feeling straight away. People walked out of their lives for good. It happened. I speak from experience. I sat down on his chair trying not to catastrophise. I told myself I was reading too much into it and probably projecting: despite appearances, Lewis wasn't me. There would be a perfectly harmless explanation for his absence: he was meeting with a friend. (Friend? What friend, he'd said yesterday. Not a single one left since his wife fell ill, never mind died. Everyone really awkward around him, they couldn't cope. Neither could he. He ended up keeping himself to himself, a relief for all involved parties. He mentioned the term compassion fatigue in respect to his friendship group, which apparently happened when things failed to get back to normal after a certain, socially prescribed length of time: should look that up.) Ok, no friend then. A trip to the shop? The fridge could certainly do with restocking. Whatever it was, he would walk through the door any minute now and show his miserable little face. Why wouldn't he. Why. I pulled my copy of *As If* out of my pocket and placed it on my lap.

I didn't read. I catastrophised. What if Lewis heard from Howe before I had the chance to explain. If Howe called or emailed in a flurry of post-audition excitement, perhaps to discuss next steps or to confirm personal details before drafting the contract, who knew how Lewis might react. What if he came straight out with it: he hadn't actually attended the audition. Best-case scenario, Howe would take it as Lewis continuing his Korine farce. Ok, 'Lindsey', she would say. She would play along, referring to the actor who had attended the audition as Lindsey Korine. Lewis would put two and two together, realising that I had showed up in his stead. He'd flip out. Renege my acceptance on the spot. Hang up the phone and not answer it again. It couldn't be: if I'd been invested before, at this point I couldn't bear the thought of him bringing to a halt what I, if not set in motion, then kept going at significant personal cost.

Four p.m. and no sign of him. I had worked myself into a state, convinced it had already happened: he'd had the phone call. He'd undone my good work. Even if he hadn't – if, say, he'd received a call he couldn't make sense of and hung up or let it ring out – the likelihood I was missing vital communications delivered to his phone was increasing by the minute. Worse, I started to worry about his physical welfare. Imagined him lying in a ditch he couldn't get out of. Head concussed and hypothermic. What if he'd done something stupid, I wouldn't put it past him. I decided that waiting around wouldn't do. I had to be more proactive. Christ, I would try to track him down. How.

I could start by visiting his mother. I knew she lived in New Cross, South East London, he'd said so himself. They were, if not close, then closer since his wife's death, apparently. But as I went through his drawers and boxes trying to locate Mrs Lewis's address, I couldn't help picturing my own mother's place, also in New Cross. If I went south, I couldn't trust myself not to head straight for the house I myself had grown up in – ex-council, Victorian terrace – and knock on the front room window as soon as I arrived. My mother would come to the door.

'Lindsey,' she would say.

'Mum.' I would bend down compliantly so she could take my face into her hands.

'How's the child,' she would ask, scrutinising me, looking for nonverbal responses she'd go on to interpret, by which I mean misinterpret. 'I wouldn't recognise him if I saw him in the street. They grow up so fast.'

This was her telling me that we as a family didn't visit as often as she imagined we should. 'He still looks like he looked like at Christmas,' I would reply.

'How's the wife?'

'She finished treatment in February.'

'Cancer gone?'

I affirmed, touching the wooden door frame.

'I imagine it isn't,' my mother would say. 'The neighbour up the road had the all-clear in November. In January, it came back in her liver. Incurable now.' After a pause: 'She hasn't got long.'

Nothing from me. Not a peep.

'No child should grow up without his mother,' she would continue.

'Well he isn't,' I would snap. 'Is he.'

This was a best-case scenario. If Laurie had called her and told her I had left, I would not hear the end of it. Point being, a visit to Lewis's mother was out of the question. Too risky. Too close to home.

Six p.m., he still hadn't returned. I entertained a range of ideas including paying his agent a visit. If I did manage to locate a name and address, who would I go as? Myself? Or Lewis? Better to look for Lewis's mobile phone number directly, then call him from a public phone box: did they still exist? Would I need coins? And who notes down their phone number anyway in this day and age? In the end, I decided that my best hope of finding him would be to patrol the neighbourhood systematically. Given his physical limitations, I could be fairly certain that he hadn't gone far. The idea was to circumnavigate a territory marked by Aldersgate Street to the east, Clerkenwell Road leading into Theobalds Road to the north, Southampton Row to the west and Holborn to the south. I would proceed to walk the smaller connecting streets and parks in between. Then I'd start over. If he sat on a park bench somewhere en route, there he would be. If he'd set up a cardboard tent the better to hide under, well, he would come out of it sooner or later. I would set off first thing tomorrow and walk for as long as it took. I was confident that the strategy would deliver results fairly quickly.

I spent what was left of the evening going through the rest of his drawers, cupboards and boxes. I confirmed what I already knew, namely that the contents of the flat, their majority, didn't belong to Lewis but rather the tenant he was subletting from. Apart from the boxed items, I didn't find anything that might offer insights regarding his person or possible whereabouts. It was worth it regardless: I found cash in a kitchen drawer. Five hundred in total. More than I'd had at my disposal in years. In it went, the whole bundle, into my coat pocket. Plenty of clothes to go around, too. (Lewis hadn't taken any. Not a jacket. Nothing against the rain, liable to start up at any point: a concern.) I considered investing in a cheap phone. I could leave a note on the table with my number. Were Lewis to return in my absence, he could call me. I never went through with it, fearing he would come back, see the number and choose not to call. I didn't want to open myself up to that sort of rejection.

I lay in his bed that night. Didn't want to miss him if he returned. (He didn't.) I couldn't sleep. At my happiest, I relived the audition, which in view of the outcome I'd reconfigured as a success in my head. At my lowest, I recited my audition piece to myself, again and again, which was the closest I came to praying: anything to stave off thoughts of Lewis in peril, or my wife and child who lest I forget I had abandoned.

A week earlier, the child had shown Laurie and me an advert on Instagram: the kitten stood up on its hind legs wearing a trapper hat with ear flaps and a little satchel over its shoulder. It looked forlorn, more where's-the-emergency-exit than capable of providing any kind of emotional support, but heart-rending nevertheless. Please, could he have it, the child said. He loved it. He loved it already. We considered it. He'd lost his light a little over the course of the last several years. You can't protect them like you want to in case of parental illness, not if it's prolonged or god forbid chronic. He'd turned hyper. He threw tantrums. He had become serious where previously he was funny. So yes, maybe a kitten would help. It arrived at the flat two days later, delivered by a bicycle courier. I received it, then sat it down on the living room floor. It jittered like a bag of leaves. The child knelt next to it, stroking it. I looked at it for a while.

'Laurie,' I said after several minutes, 'I'm going to return it.'

'Why what's wrong with it.'

Come on, Laurie, I didn't say. The kitten looked like it had fallen into a garden fork: one of its eyes was missing. In its place was a days' old injury which didn't appear to be healing.

'I want to hear you say it,' Laurie said. 'What, in your view, is wrong with the kitten, Lindsey.'

'I don't want it in the flat,' I said. It is damaged goods, I didn't say.

I didn't need to. Just like Laurie did not need to say that she herself, by some, might be considered damaged goods: myself included, apparently.

Maybe she wasn't, but I was surprised that what seemed like a watershed moment in our relationship happened so naturally, irrevocably and without warning at the exact point when things were starting to look up. I wouldn't go so far as to say that either Laurie or myself were back to our former selves – we had no expectations to ever be – but we were in the process of reclaiming a sense of normality. Laurie had returned to work, was regaining her strength, and she was not going to tolerate a husband, me, whose response to her or anyone else with a disability, chronic disease or physical difference was anything other than unambivalent support. Who was the liability here, she appeared to be asking, suggesting it wasn't her or the kitten, but me.

'Why don't you take the kitten,' Laurie said, 'and return it. Or exchange it for another. One without history.'

'I will, too,' I said, injecting fake optimism into my voice and demeanour to mitigate what felt like the finality of my subsequent behaviour. Pretending that a tectonic shift in the relationship, a betrayal, wasn't occurring, I took my exit cue: 'Consider it done.'

With that, I swiped up the kitten with one hand, instinctively held it as far away from my person as I could and made for the door. I was in no shape to embark on any sort of journey beyond taking the rubbish out: I was wearing pyjama bottoms and a washed-out white t-shirt saying *Straight Outta Money* in the 'Straight Outta Compton' typeface. And yet, I didn't stop to collect my jacket nor to exchange my sliders for trainers. I left my phone and keys on the kitchen table and, no other way of saying it, fled. The child followed me as far as the landing, eyes like headlights I imagine: I didn't look back.

I didn't trust myself to evaluate the events that

had led to my departure. Two versions coexisted in my mind: in the first, I'm-going-to-return-the-kitten was my own personal I'm-popping-out-to-the-shop-for-a-pint-of-milk. This was the version in which I refused the parameters of my life as I knew it and in a sense broke with myself: I walked out under a pretext intending to never return. In the other version, Laurie finally, rightly, kicked me out: god knows I had it coming. The truth was probably somewhere in between: after everything that had happened, we found ourselves in a state of defeat in which neither could help the other. Our child? On the receiving end of it all through no fault of his own. Stepping out onto Golden Lane, with kitten, I turned right. I could've taken any direction: what mattered was the walking, the walking away from what had been too much for too long, and the particular manner in which I was carrying the kitten: I insisted on keeping it at arm's length as if it were cursed and/or contagious. I was holding it around its chest in a gentle fist lest I crush its ribcage. Its front paws rested on the soft part between my index finger and thumb and its hind legs and tail dangled above the pavement ahead of me. To an extent, I envied it: it was the happiest living being far and wide. I didn't return it like I said

I would. Instead, I freed or abandoned it in the small park just east of the estate. As soon as I sat it down on the wet grass, it flung itself into the bushes almost wantonly. I was aware I was leaving it at the mercy of an unstable environment it knew little to nothing about: add that to my existing guilt. What difference did it make: I was beyond redemption as it was. I left the park and went on to walk the streets without destination for I don't know how long. It got dark once or twice. When the rain turned heavier, I sought shelter in the Barbican underpass where I, eventually, saw and chose Lewis. I found that the context explained a thing or two, the extent of my investment in Lewis's affairs, for starters: in view of my own irremediable situation, I felt like my life depended on fixing, or at the very least making a difference to, Lewis's.

In the morning, I packed a little sandwich in cling film, and some biscuits. I found a repurposable container which I filled with tap water. I retired the Oslos for now, on account of their resistance to wearing in. Back in my sliders, coated and wax jacketed, I set off in hope.

My plan to find Lewis came apart as soon as I put

it into practice. As I passed Holborn Library my left leg gave way. My thorax had different ideas: it went out the other way. Why I thought I was capable of describing an ambitious trajectory on foot and unaided, having tracked to The Cut and back the day before, I didn't know. I changed tack there and then: instead of patrolling the area, I would take up position outside the library. I could do a lot worse: the swooping concrete canopy above the main entrance felt inviting and the location would work from a strategic point of view. Theobalds Road was a main artery for pedestrian traffic, Lewis was bound to pass sooner or later. On the other side of the road was a small public garden whose name I forget but that I imagined he might sit in. I found a scrap of cardboard which I laid out, not under the canopy, but out of the way, at the bottom of a ramp leading up to the entrance. I sat on it relatively comfortably. If I bent forward and turned right, I could see hundreds of metres to the west. If I turned left, to the east. I was pleased with myself, enjoying the unexpectedly milder, drier weather, when one of the library staff came out of the building. If I insisted on sitting there, she said, could I please pull up my legs rather than stretch them across the width of the pavement. I was creating a trip hazard for passers-by including library patrons. Worse, I was blocking access to their accessibility ramp, defying its purpose. I'd never been on bad terms with library staff before, so I did my best to comply. If I was going to be here for the long haul, by which I meant all day, I needed the staff on side. Had I known just how long the haul would turn out to be, I might have fought harder for my right to position my legs in whichever way best supported my overall frame and posture. I would've saved myself a world of physical pain.

I had enough to contend with psychologically: despite my efforts, I did not see Lewis once in the two-week period that followed. How. I'd had the thought he might not want to be found. I even considered the possibility that I had motivated his departure in the first place: his expressions, his refusal to engage with me or even acknowledge my presence that last morning gave me reason to suspect it. Not the first time I'd provoked a negative reaction. Some members of the public, even now, didn't reciprocate when I smiled and made eye contact. Sending friendliness into the world to have it backfire, a daily occurrence for me. It wasn't unthinkable that Lewis had worked out my daily routine and made use of his flat in my absence. What if he waited in the bus shelter outside Barbican station, say, and watched me leave in the morning. Once I'd cleared out, he'd go in, then leave before my return at seven or eight. On day three, I started searching the flat for signs of his presence. If he ever came in, he never once used the shower. He never lay in the bed. I took to attaching a single hair to the front door and frame every morning: if the hair were disturbed on my return, I would know he'd been in, or so went the theory. Not once did the hair stay in place, however: an indication of the high levels of condensation in the communal staircase, rather than a potential trespasser. I was so preoccupied thinking up versions of Lewis's life post-disappearance that sometimes, when I kept watch, I caught myself not even looking at the world or whatever it threw at me. As late May turned into June, I'd as good as given up hope of ever seeing him again.

The first time I did see him was on Tuesday, the fourth of June, early afternoon. I was on my way to my usual spot when I saw him stride in the direction I was coming from on the other side of the road. He was in his regular tracksuit – or just his track top, was it, and black cotton trousers, white socks flashing below the hems. I noticed an earring, that was new. It happened so fast, so unexpectedly, I didn't know what to think or how to react. How, in all this time I'd been looking for him, I had failed to establish a course of action should I encounter him, you tell me. In the moment, I entertained the following options: Hiding. Should I hide? Or should I approach him or otherwise draw his attention to me, e.g. wave? It might make matters worse: he might panic and disappear more thoroughly. Avoid daylight henceforth. If there was any chance he didn't know I was after him, I would prefer to keep it that way. By now, he had passed me. He was in fact increasing the distance between us. To confirm: he wasn't actually in his track top, but in a pale brown blazer. I didn't stop to think what it meant. I went in pursuit. I injured my good foot in the process: the pavements at this historico-political juncture were littered with potholes, loose paving slabs. I stopped at the corner of Theobalds and Gray's Inn Road, propping myself up at a small round table outside a cafe, which, unbalanced, tipped over. We went down together. An employee came out, which gave me the impetus I needed to get myself up. But by the time I turned into Gray's Inn Road, I was too late. No Lewis far and wide. I had lost him.

I can't overstate the impact the incident had on me. I'd sprained my right ankle, but other than that, I wasn't physically worse off than before. Yet my confidence was severely dented: my lack of forward planning had cost me dearly. At least Lewis was alive, I took comfort in that. Judging from what little I'd seen I wouldn't say he was well, but he was out there and covering ground. No reason why I shouldn't happen upon him again.

I was reading a lot during this period. I'd found more books in Lewis's boxes – novels and plays, as well as acting textbooks – which I'd stacked up on the table. I spent my evenings and nights working my way through them: preferable to engaging in my own spiralling thought processes. At first I read indiscriminately. Then I found myself picking up where I left off the morning before the audition, prioritising the textbooks and *As If*. I always returned to *As If*. I thought there were layers to it.

I might have been overly keen to correct my mistake: over the subsequent days, I spent an inordinate length of time shadowing a guy who looked like Lewis. In hindsight, I suspected it was the actor I had met in the National Theatre Rehearsal Studio, who I kept telling myself was lined up for the role as my,

Lewis's, understudy in *As If*, the series. In reality, there was no way of knowing if Howe hadn't invited him, too, to audition for the lead, which would make him some sort of rival. Jelley, was it. His name was Lucien, pronounced Loo-shn, Jelley. Anyway, he who looked like Lewis, who I thought was Lewis, who I wanted, desperately, to be␣Lewis and who I couldn't be sure wasn't Lewis, came out of Holborn Library around midday on the sixth of June and turned left. He wore brown corduroys held up by a belt, and a novelty t-shirt of the sort I myself favoured and used to wear to amuse myself and my child. He carried an unbranded plastic bag. I got up and did what I'd been planning on doing since failing to capitalise on the previous sighting: I followed him discreetly and without hesitation. If he noticed me he didn't show it. He neither sped up nor slowed down. The guy who I assumed to be Lewis went into a cafe, Ludo's, at the bottom of Gray's Inn Road. Me in his slipstream. I'd not been in here before: twenty or so wooden tables, the typical condiments on each: salt and pepper shakers, sugar pourer, ketchup and brown sauce plastic squeeze bottles. Fake-leather-bound menus, not a tablecloth far and wide. Maroon and white chequered lino tiles on the floor and framed celebrity photos all over the walls: some signed and dedicated to Ludo's owners and staff. It wasn't busy. The man I had down as Lewis took a seat at a window table by himself. I sat down at the table facing him. If he noticed me, he didn't show it. He waved over the waiter who he seemed friendly with and ordered eggs on toast. When his food arrived minutes later, he thanked the waiter and placed a napkin onto his lap to protect his corduroys. Next, he squirted ketchup onto his plate and proceeded to swipe it up with his eggs on toast, the part he'd cut and put his fork in, leaving white porcelain trails. Only then did I begin seriously to suspect that the man at the table opposite me was not Lewis at all: I'd only ever seen him eat digestive biscuits, a piece of fruit, or, more likely, not a thing. Seeing this guy push his egg float across the plate brought the doubts I may or may not have had on account of the corduroys and the t-shirt into focus. 'I'll have what he has,' I said, loudly, to the waiter who had been ignoring me. The waiter did a double take – looking from me to Jelley, then to me again – and nodded. Coming up. Hearing my voice, Jelley stopped chewing and briefly looked up. Without showing any signs of recognition, he resumed labouring his toast. If the former was in keeping with Lewis's behaviour on the morning he left, what he did next was entirely out of character. He pulled a children's toy, a little monkey with puffy cheeks, a Monchhichi, I believed, out of the plastic bag. Something pink, the tip of a pencil perhaps, was stuck in its mouth, those monkeys have a hole where their mouth is, I knew because my child had one just like it. Lewis tried to remove the pink lead with the leftmost prong of his fork, pressuring the little thing in the mouth, twisting, boring. Watch out or you'll injure the cheek! I barely stopped myself from intervening. If you scratch its eye, you won't hear the end of it. As if he had heard me, he let up. Inspected what looked like the mending of the toy's leg instead. Satisfied, he replaced it into the carrier bag. Then he waved over the waiter and paid up. Unlike Lucien Jelley, I did not have an appetite. I got up as soon as I settled my own bill, my plate untouched. By the time I'd convinced the waiter that no, I did not want him to put the food in a takeaway bag for me, I'd lost my target. Maybe I'd already decided I wouldn't follow him. If he wasn't Lewis, what would be the point.

I called it a day and returned to the flat early. As soon as I sat down, the thought started to haunt me that the corduroyed man in the cafe might have been Lewis after all. What if I'd rationalised away the clear similarities, forcing the understudy explanation out of a fear of confrontation? What if, somewhere, I'd rather not know what Lewis would say to me given the chance? Even if the man I had followed really was Jelley, had I not left important questions unasked? Being an actor himself, he was part of the same professional networks and cultures: surely he would have insights relating to, if not Lewis's whereabouts, then at least his headspace. Either way, Jelley was a lead worth pursuing.

The next day, I returned to Ludo's. I ordered eggs on toast. I waited for hours. If I was burning through my budget, I thought, eating out, I'd better have something to show for it. By the end of my shift, he hadn't turned up. The day after that, he did. That Saturday, I arrived at ten in the morning in case he was early. I ordered 'the usual', which I proceeded to nibble on every half hour or so to make it last. By the time Jelley arrived at around noon, the eggs on my plate were cold, the toast had solidified. Disconcertingly, I noticed a paperback, azure blue and light brown, sticking out of the back pocket of his corduroys: *As If*. A provocation if ever I saw one. He made for his regular table and, pulling the paperback out of his pocket, sat down.

He started reading. I got up at once and carried my plate over to him.

'May I?'

Looking up from his book, Jelley gestured to sit on the chair facing him. He had noticed me the day before yesterday, he said. How could he not. The resemblance was striking.

I asked if he was an actor.

'No,' he said, or 'Not anymore,' I didn't quite catch that. He was a stay-at-home parent. I didn't believe him.

'What are you reading.'

'Oh this,' he said. 'Nothing.' He closed his copy of *As If*, put it on the table and covered it up with his napkin.

'I was recently cast as the lead in the TV adaptation,' I said, to gauge his response.

He looked me in the eye for what felt like too long. Then he started laughing, quietly at first. Then he laughed so loud that the waiter came over and asked if everything was ok. I waved him away.

'You don't say,' Jelley said once he'd composed himself. 'I imagined him differently.'

'Who.'

'The main character. Cyril.'

'Different how.'

'Just different.'

'Well, I'm an actor,' I said. 'He won't be like me. That's the whole point.'

'You must be excellent at what you do,' he said as if amused. As if the exchange were entertaining to him. Then his food arrived. He tucked into it straight away, chewing, steering his egg toast ship through a sea of ketchup, blithely, carefree.

I couldn't think how to bring up Lewis after that. And what would be the point. If he had lied to me about who he was, why would he be honest about anything else. I took my napkin and placed it onto my half-empty plate. I didn't particularly like eggs on toast and I wanted him to know. Then I got up and left.

I felt I'd run out of track after that. Over the following fortnight, I increasingly lost focus. I neglected the search effort, visiting the library only rarely. When I did, I occupied maximum space by the ramp so that the staff would come out and talk to me. I'd devised a whole spiel to extend these small interactions and yet they always ended so soon. For the most part, I was on my own. I stayed in the flat a lot. I was still reading, still preparing for the day when Lewis would return and we'd finally turn our focus to acting: wishful thinking, I suppose. Actually, I was fully aware that the longer Lewis was AWOL, the more urgent my initially possibly exaggerated concerns became. By now, he would've received direct communications from Howe and her team, I was certain of it – text messages, emails – without the mitigation an explanation from me might have offered. He would have had plenty of opportunity to clear up the 'misunderstanding' and count himself out. He might have done nothing at all: if he didn't sign the contract that, if I understood correctly, would've come through to him via his agent, he would've brought his involvement in the production and mine by extension to a halt without lifting a finger. Chances were, I'd been flogging a dead horse for a while.

I got in my head at this juncture. Specifically, I struggled to reconcile to the fact that nothing I'd done had brought me closer to Lewis. Why not. Where was he. It didn't make any sense. At my lowest, I got hung up on the idea I had made Lewis up. That he never existed. What if, over the last several years, I had lived with the possibility of my wife's death so intently that I had invented a version of myself who was actually bereaved. In the state I was in, it seemed plausible that this particular part of my self should have taken on a life of its, his, own: Aubrey Lewis. Even when Laurie went into remission, the spectre of her death never went anywhere. It lived rent-free in my head as they say. If I had tried to outrun it by leaving her – if that was in fact a more honest reason why I'd left – there it was, doubling down, giving itself a name, Lewis. Another facet of him, Lewis, was informed by what I recognised as a midlife crisis. Strange how existential upheavals could, once named, sound almost trivial: putting words to experience, like acting, required a lot more skill than it seemed. Long way of saying, I had come to admit to myself that I had certain regrets regarding my life choices. I never used to. Didn't think I did anyway. Lewis being the actor I never was, how was that a coincidence. In what world.

If I came to my senses, if I arrived at the conclusion that Lewis was real after all, it was because I couldn't explain away the fact I was living in a flat that wasn't mine. Whose flat but Lewis's? Whose clothes was I wearing, or whose sublessor's clothes: the beige tracksuit had disappeared with him, of course. Who was that in the poster on my wall, reliably looking down on me. Who played Schmidt in *People*, and who was the boy in the schoolyard thirty-five years ago, impressing me more than I'd realised. Most importantly, whose career was I trying to sustain in their absence, or, if I were honest with myself, trying to piggyback on? On the back of whose achievements had I got myself in front of a high-profile director in the first place? Based on these and other tangible facts, I did away with the thought that I'd invented Lewis. As a matter of fact, I classified it as intrusive. If I was losing my mind, it was this sort of self-doubt that was doing it, not Aubrey Lewis. It was this sort of inward-directed perspective that made me interpret other people in relation to my own concerns and problems: not something I was in the habit of doing or even subscribed to.

Imagine my surprise when the screenplay, *As If*, came through the post. I'm not exaggerating when I say that seeing the physical, bound script and imagining the possibilities it entailed remade me as a person. It refocused me instantly. I put an end to what was left of my four-week search effort and concentrated on preparing the part of Cyril instead. I'm not sure at which point exactly I took the mental and emotional step that promoted me from Lewis's assistant to leading actor. Maybe when I saw Lucien Jelley in Ludo's cafe, or while performing for Howe at the National Theatre Rehearsal Studio, or when first I decided to attend the audition in Lewis's stead, or when I chose him that night in the underpass, or when I was eleven years old, watching Gary Oldman at work. It had been building, I suppose. The countless hours of reading and practising I had done this last month also played a role. Long way of saying, I decided to participate in the read-through, scheduled for the twenty-eighth of June, and the shoot after that if they'd let me. If Lewis wasn't up to it, I was.

6

It was never about going anywhere in particular. It was always about walking away from Korine and the flat he'd made intolerable through his presence. So I walked, circuiting an area defined by my physical capabilities: northbound on Aldersgate Street, then left into Clerkenwell Road leading into Theobalds Road, then left into Southampton Row and left again into Holborn. What a propellant fear was, I marvelled as I proceeded to range the smaller connecting streets and public gardens in the circumscribed territory. The walking worked: at no point did I see people who weren't there, at least not to my knowledge. No Korine far and wide. At nightfall, I sought shelter under a bench in a public garden I don't recall the name of, just off Theobalds Road. I was woken up by a couple of men, neither of whom was Korine, pulling me out from under the bench, one leg each.

I had no reason to believe that either of them knew who I was, yet they were offended enough by my presence to kick me in the ribcage repeatedly. Then they just left me there. Let the precipitation and the relative cold do the rest. At dawn, thoughts of Korine, even Howe, coming into my head, I tried to get up to resume my rounds thus distracting myself. I had to concede that I wasn't in the condition to. So I made my way – how! – to the Barbican underpass, which I felt offered a modicum of protection compared to the open air. I spent a day or two sitting there, leaning against the internal cladding, a spectrum of sand-related colours which, meditated on, worked as a sedative. Having zipped my track top all the way up, freezing, I was waiting for my injuries to heal or stop hurting enough for me to get on my way. It was here that I was approached by a woman holding a child by the hand.

'Lindsey,' the woman said. 'What are you doing.'

'Aubrey,' I corrected her. 'Aubrey Lewis. Pleased to meet you.' I held out my hand. The woman ignored it.

'How long have you been sitting here. I thought you were at your mother's.'

At this point the child started to cry, responding

to his mother's tone, or else the sight of me, hard to tell which.

'Not long,' I said in response to her question. 'I never,' I added, apropos her supposition.

Two things: one, I knew at once that the woman was Korine's wife. (She'd called me Lindsey, for starters.) What did the fact she existed – if indeed she did, my perceptive faculties weren't exactly reliable lately – mean in respect to Korine, a figment of my imagination as far as I was concerned? My thought process was cut short by the realisation that, two, Korine's wife didn't not look like Laurie, my dead wife. On the day, she wore light blue joggers and a washed-out black t-shirt with cap sleeves. Her hair was shortish and growing. Seeing me, that is, 'Lindsey', she seemed upset and serious and kind and irritated at the same time.

'Get off the floor,' Korine's wife said. 'Jesus Christ, Lindsey.'

'Don't cry,' I said to the child, which made him hysterical.

'Dad's fine,' Korine's wife said to the child. 'He will be fine.'

Before I could do anything to prevent it, the child broke free, ran towards me and threw his little arms round my neck. I tentatively patted his back, there, there, which both the child and Korine's wife appeared to approve of. I stroked the back of his head. There.

'Come on then. Let's go,' Korine's wife said.

I looked at her quizzically.

Yes, she signalled. Get up. What are you waiting for.

The child and I let go of each other. I rose with some difficulty, hoping it wouldn't come across as reluctant. I dusted my trousers off to middling success. I made to tuck in my track top which had come undone somewhere down the line. The child stared so I stopped. Korine's wife started moving eastwards along the underpass. The child and I followed. He took my hand and skipped and sang. Some strange song I'd never heard before.

'What happened to you,' Korine's wife said when she noticed my ribcage, the condition of which impacted my ability to walk without drawing attention.

I told her I had been attacked, but that some of my injuries, physical and psychological, preceded the event.

'Attack, what attack,' Korine's wife asked.

It wasn't important. I'd been miserable and, now that I had an invitation to come-with to hold on to, I wasn't going to get side tracked by non-issues. We turned out of the underpass and into Golden Lane. To the left, the familiar housing estate. Despite the proximity to my Aldersgate Street sublet I had avoided the Golden Lane Estate since I'd moved out two years prior. The one-bed top-floor flat Laurie and I used to rent in Stanley Cohen House? I could see it up there. An unusual flower had appeared in the window, placed there by the current tenant, I imagined.

We turned into the entrance block to one of the neighbouring low-rise buildings, Basterfield House. I noted that, despite the residents' association's long-term campaign for better upkeep, the place still looked dilapidated: whatever funds were available were invested elsewhere: the public-facing Barbican Estate down the road, I suspected, no change there. We went up the stairs and along the corridor connecting to the maisonettes spreading across the raised ground and second floors. Before long, Korine's wife stopped at one of the front doors, which she unlocked. Inside, the child took off his shoes, ran into the living room and up the internal stairs leading to the bedrooms no doubt. Korine's wife said to make myself at home, she wouldn't be long. Then she followed the child.

I sat down on the sofa, trying to orientate myself. The flat felt nice: lived in, done on a budget. Not huge, but the living room was double-height. Laurie and I used to look at these from our balcony: the pretty maroon cladding under the upper windows, the expansive glass frontage overlooking the communal gardens. We meant to try for one for years. Upgrade. We never got round to it. Now I was in one, looking out. In the state I was in, the effect was giddying.

Korine's wife returned minutes later. She picked up some toys from the floor, then sat down on a chair facing me. 'He's asleep,' she said. In his own bed. He hadn't been sleeping in his own bed since I left. She barely managed to get him to go to school in the morning. He insisted on staying at home in case I returned. I felt the need to apologise. She shrugged. She wasn't in the mood for excuses. In fact, she would go to bed herself. Early start tomorrow. 'You can stay in the spare room,' Korine's wife said. 'Help yourself to whatever.' With that, she left me to it.

I went into the tiny kitchen at the back of the

living room. I opened every cupboard to locate a plate and cutlery before going into the fridge. I found bread which I sliced and buttered and ate standing up. I found some paracetamol, too, which I took with a little tap water. I didn't know what I'd done to deserve it, but I decided not to question Korine's wife's hospitality. I did not have the luxury to. If there had been a mistake, I'd rectify it in the morning. Minutes later, I went upstairs.

The spare room was central-London small: once the guest bed was unfolded there was little space to move around it. The bed itself was too short for me, but the sheets were cotton and the pillow capable of supporting my neck. I tend to sleep through anything, but that evening I lay awake in the relative dark, trying to make sense of what was happening to me. I should have been contending with the fact that, clearly, Lindsey Korine was not as imaginary as I'd assumed him to be. These here were his wife and young child. This was his flat, or the flat he used to live in: I got the sense she was paying for it. In any case, Korine was a person, a husband who'd either left the family he didn't deserve in the first place, or, more likely, been asked to leave. But I wasn't in a position to re-evaluate anything, least of all Korine's ontological status: its implications for me, positives, negatives. Instead, I felt like a dead leaf on springs, meaning a strange mechanism kept me going, resisting environmental forces – goings-on I barely understood – and fighting, in an understated way, for my life.

Then the door opened and the child came in. He stood in front of my bed, light entering from the landing. Could he come in.

'What, the bed? No,' I said.

He was holding a toy monkey with silicone cheeks and a hole for a mouth. Stuffing came out of a tear in its leg. His monkey was sick, he said. Its hair was falling out through its knee. It had to flush the toilet twice to protect the child in the house from the toxic waste it produced on account of its medical treatment.

'I see,' I said. 'What about your mum. Where is your mum?' I meant to say 'where' but I might have said 'how'.

Apparently, his mum was in remission. He said it with the   ult.

'I hav   , while you're at school, I'll take   y hospital where they'll fix him.

'I don't know,' the child said, looking at the monkey, silently consulting with it. 'Ok fine.'

I got up and – past Korine's wife's bedroom – took the child back to his room. He climbed into bed and looked at me expectantly. If he noticed that I didn't know his routine, he didn't play up. On the contrary: he guided me through it. You take this book over there, he said, pointing. No, next to it. Uh-huh. You sit at the edge of my bed. Not that far away! He giggled. First, you read the part where et cetera. Then, you start from the beginning. I followed his instructions to a T. At one point, he looked like he'd fallen asleep. But as soon as I stopped reading, he opened his eyes. You have to read until I'm asleep. It won't work otherwise. What won't work. He was trying to dream of something or other, a prerequisite, apparently, of it happening in real life. Like the kid in the book? Obviously. Not many pictures inside the book, I thought. Sinister undertones and difficult for the age group. Showed what I knew.

'When you go, leave the small light on and the door open,' the child said. 'C

'Don't say capeesh,

'Why not?'

'It's not nice.'

Fact was, she would come and go at unusual hours. She would go tight-lipped on the rare occasions when the conversation turned to her work. She mentioned a partner, Sally, and a superior, Sean. If I were honest, I didn't quite get what she did on a day-to-day basis and she wasn't going to fill me in. I further learnt that Korine's wife had undergone treatment for a rare form of lymphoma over the last several years. The child had been right: she was in remission. When first I had it confirmed she'd had cancer, I had an almost immobilising sense of please-not-again. Don't do this to me, I pleaded with no one in particular. I kept telling myself this was different to what I'd lived through before: Korine's wife's prognosis was good. I touched wood as soon as I had the thought to frustrate its jinxy potential.

If I didn't already, I started to suspect – no, I understood, Korine's wife let me know in not as many words – that she knew very well I wasn't Korine. She was inviting me to enter into a tacit agreement for the child's sake – and for hers, too. Over the last few years, she had managed to hold down a demanding role despite her illness. She did what she could to take care of herself, but she had yet to recover her pre-cancer strength and stamina. Her phased return to work,

So-and-so from school said capeesh.
'I don't care,' I said, then did as I was told.

At the breakfast table, the child insisted on sitting on my lap. He was singing again, the same crazy-making song. There was coffee. Cornflakes and fruit. Korine's wife was dressed and on her way out. She wore the same light blue joggers she'd worn the previous day, this time paired with a men's shirt and a pink and brown windbreaker with elasticated waist.

'No need to drop him at school,' she said, taking her keys. 'The neighbour is picking him up. But if you could collect him? See you later?'

'Where are you going?'

'Work, where else.'

I wondered what sort of employer let her dress in what was technically leisurewear. Laurie used to favour clothes not unlike hers: she'd taught at an arts college.

Over the next day or two, I gathered from what minimal information Korine's wife let slip that she worked either as a private investigator or for the government: national security, specifically intelligence-gathering. A desk job, I told myself, it had to be: fieldwork was hard to imagine, that one step too far.

so-called, a legal entitlement, was phased in name more than in practice. She could do with a modicum of support at home. This suited me: almost by default, I fell into actor mode. For all intents and purposes, I started to play Korine. I approached 'Korine' like I approached any high-stakes acting role. Instinctively, I'd already adopted some of his mannerisms: His way of touching his lips when he was thinking. His way of throwing his legs over every armrest available while sitting. I walked taller. I laughed more often and more loudly. I tried not to ever take no for an answer and I listened with one ear only when anybody was talking. I started dressing differently, too. Most of the clothes I found in Korine's wardrobe didn't work for me aesthetically. But he did have a pair of those trainers with the N on, the exact trainers I used to wear before I rejected them, and a pair of reasonably cut corduroys. They were too long in the leg, but hardly: if I held them up with a belt, the hem sat neatly on top of my ankle. There was a jean jacket with sherpa lining and collar which I could work with. I even borrowed one of his t-shirts, depicting a cat lying flat on its back, the slogan *this is how your email finds me* underneath. The child practically died laughing when he saw it. He wouldn't calm down.

He was in on it, too. After Korine's wife left the flat that first morning, he communicated his routine to me like he'd taught me how to put him to bed. He stood on a chair like a mini conductor, pointing at various cupboards, the exact locations where his food containers and snack items were stored. If he was playing me – *two* packs of fruit gummies? – I allowed it. He even led me to his friend's house for a playdate later that day. We missed a turning and got there late. But overall, a valiant effort.

By day five, I had the school run down pat. After the first week, I knew the entire routine: Korine's wife would work long and unpredictable hours, including at the weekend. I would stay in the flat in the mornings, clear up, enjoy the light and the view of the garden, then, on weekdays, pick up the child from school in the afternoon. I'd take him to the playground – usually locally, Fortune Street Park – or to one of his regular activities. His favourite: baby chess. Strange boy, Cyril was. The child's name was Cyril, did I say.

At some point in week two, I started fabricating false memories involving Korine's wife and child: Cyril's first day in nursery school was a debacle, they called to have him picked up early; the uneasy relationship I had with my, Korine's, mother had wide-ranging implications for Korine's wife's and my marriage; on our second date, I took Korine's wife for a walk round Victoria Park, it was pissing down. The conversations with Korine's wife helped: she would dispense pieces of information as they came up. She communicated, in a roundabout way, any relationship dynamics I needed to be aware of to navigate day-to-day life. But primarily, I based my performance on a combination of what I myself had seen of Korine (enough) and the fact I was navigating a set of conditions which, taken together, amounted to Korine's life and produced Korine-like responses. If acting was indeed living truthfully under imaginary circumstances, I had the advantage that on this occasion said circumstances were real.

Not that I didn't get it wrong. I frequently did Korine incorrectly. Like the time I neglected to mispronounce Cyril's teacher's Korean name which I gathered Korine did without fail. Or when I chatted to his wife's mother on the landline and enjoyed it, rather than let it ring out: I could tell from her response that Korine would never. Ironically, there seemed to be an understanding between Korine's wife and myself that the changes – the differences between myself and Korine, or I should say my interpretation of Korine and Korine as she knew him – were to be welcomed. In other words, Korine's wife preferred me to Korine. The child did, too.

On the evening of day ten or eleven, Laurie and I sat at opposite ends of the sofa, Cyril on the carpet in front of us, watching TV. (I'd started calling Korine's wife by her name, which was Laurie, of all names. She continued to address me as Lindsey, which I was grateful for.) As it happened, Laurie liked to watch *People* on BBC iPlayer before bed: she found the repetitiveness, the ritual nature of her viewing, relaxing. As usual, Laurie and Cyril laughed at the exact same places and, strangely, so did I. At some point during Schmidt's five-minute appearance in the episode, Laurie, without taking her eyes off the screen, moved her hand across the sofa and put it into mine as if it were the most natural thing in the world. It took every bit of my acting proficiency to stay in character and, as Korine, react as if the ground hadn't just moved.

After a couple of weeks in Basterfield House, I resumed frequenting Ludo's on Gray's Inn Road. Why? Old habits, I suppose: I'd been eating at Ludo's every weekday since Laurie had died: a routine to get me out of the flat more than anything. Maybe I needed a short break from playing Korine. Maybe it was my way of checking in on Aubrey Lewis in a controlled environment: however relieved I was to see the back of the tracksuited guy, I had some awareness I was losing him faster than was probably healthy. To think how easy the tracksuit had come off: the foundation of my personality for many months, now discarded at the back of Korine's wardrobe. I'd come to see it for the band-aid it was.

I saw Korine in the cafe twice. First time, he sat alone at a table facing me. He ordered what I had. As strange as it may seem given I was slipping into his former life, I hadn't thought much about Korine, the person, at all. Instead, I'd somehow upheld his imaginary status, or modified it, in the sense that I'd turned him into a part or a character I happened to play. Now here he was, out in the world and, for all I knew, with an agenda. I witnessed the waiter converse with him, albeit reluctantly. If I continued to be under any illusions, here was my proof: he was as real as they come; part of a consensual reality people perceived and interacted with. I fell back into my strategy of ignoring him, hoping he would go away: as ineffectual now as it was then. Eating my eggs on toast, watching him from the corner of my eye, I'd say he looked worse than when last I saw him: as if he were afflicted with one of those Victorian diseases like typhoid or TB. At the same time, it seemed as though he took up the space of two or more people, such was his aptitude for making an impression on me. Why was he here? Not a coincidence, surely. Had I mentioned the waiter on the night we met? Ludo – I didn't know if this was his real name or the name I'd been calling him in my head – who was the closest thing to a friend I had left after losing my wife. What if Korine was here to ask me to vacate his life. This was assuming he knew I'd moved in with his wife and child: why wouldn't he, we weren't hiding. This is a polite heads-up, he might say. Thanks, Lewis, for deputising while I was indisposed. While I was doing whatever I was doing, throwing your flat into disarray. Now I am ready to reclaim my life. Any moment he might look up and speak it across the room. Or he might get up, approach my table and put his fist on it. Cutlery clanging from the sheer impact and strength of feeling.

None of it happened. Korine stayed at his table.

If anything, he seemed fixated on Cyril's toy, the monkey, which I'd collected earlier that day from a tailor who'd fixed the hole in its leg. For a while, we were eyeing each other like feuding dogs. I looked away first. I finished my lunch and left the premises.

Half an hour later, I stood outside Cyril's school waiting for him to come out. As per usual I stayed away from the other parents, thinking they'd know a novice at parenting minutes into a conversation. A picture of normality on the surface, I was barely holding it together. If Korine hadn't come to the cafe for the explicit purpose of warning me off, who said that a coincidental encounter wouldn't give him this exact idea. Why would he bother with a heads-up at all? The expectation seemed laughably optimistic in hindsight: what *was* there to stop him from showing up at Basterfield House unannounced and making me leave under duress. He was taller than me, more unhinged and, as far as I could tell, confrontational: he could take me in a fight, no question about it. Alternatively, he could bring my new life to an end without any effort at all: Laurie and my tacit agreement to not speak the elephant in the room, well, Korine would force us to speak it. With what consequences. With what unforeseeable consequences.

What effects would unmitigated candour about my identity have on my child, it didn't bear thinking about. (I had started referring to his child as 'my child', or 'my son'.) I wasn't prepared to return to the Aldersgate Street sublet either. Get back in the tracksuit? Not an option. I tried my best to register this as a positive: for the first time since my wife's death I had something worth defending. There was Cyril now, skipping towards me, shrieking at the top of his lungs at the sight of me, or else the toy I was holding out, good as new.

The day after, a minor crisis occurred at home: Cyril came back from school early, dragging his right foot. At first I thought he was copying my gait, an act of father/child identification, which thrilled me. But he wasn't. On the first day of wearing a new pair of sandals to school, he'd torn one of the straps. Laurie, who was working from home that day, was less than enthusiastic seeing him home already.

'That's another thirty pounds to replace the sandals,' she said frustratedly.

Her response seemed out of proportion. Made me wonder whether she was – we were, as a family – pressured financially.

Meanwhile the child started to cry and, quite unexpectedly, beg for a holiday. He took both Laurie's and my hands and announced that he wanted, no, dreamed of, a family holiday in Mallorca. He had seen an advert on TV. He wished to make lifelong memories.

'Maybe Bognor Regis,' Laurie said, looking at me.

Why not. I consented nonverbally. It'd been years since I'd been anywhere.

'When?' The child appeared to settle for the idea of Bognor Regis.

'In the autumn,' Laurie said. 'Off-season. It's cheaper.'

Satisfied, he let go of our hands. Got down on his knees and proceeded to push a toy car across the floor in one sandal.

'Laurie,' I said. 'Let's talk.'

She admitted that money was tight. She was on a decent salary, but the price hike on literally everything and the financial black hole that Kor— She cut herself short there, it all added up.

The financial black hole that Korine had been historically, I completed her sentence in my head. Got it. I committed to contributing to the rent on a monthly basis, starting now and backdated. I would've been ashamed it had taken me weeks to offer had I not put it under the rubric of me playing Korine: a reflection of his self-involved, near-parasitic modus operandi.

'And how will you do that,' Laurie said, rhetorical question.

'Leave it with me.'

No question that the expenditure, on top of the rent I continued to pay on the Aldersgate Street sublet, would eat into what was left of my savings. If I wanted to stay on top of my commitments I needed to increase my income or reduce my outgoings, ideally both. The bare expenses, eggs-toast-and-ketchup sort of life I had led as a widower no longer cut it. I had to bite my tongue a few times watching *People*, to stop myself from telling Laurie about *As If*, the forthcoming remake. Other than that, this was the first time for a while that I thought about Cyril, the role I'd turned down. It came with a generous pay package. Surely that ship had sailed when I missed the audition. It wasn't like I'd heard from Howe: she hadn't been chasing me when I went ghost. I discounted the idea of getting involved belatedly and yet I went and got the paperback out from the library the next day to finally have a look. Why, curiosity, I supposed. Strange that my sense of curiosity should be returning: I thought I had lost it for good.

Meanwhile the thought of Korine – the person, out in the world – wouldn't leave me alone. I tried to convince myself I was overreacting: nothing had come of the encounter at Ludo's two days earlier. I'd not seen him again, certainly nowhere near Basterfield House. But I remained on high alert. I couldn't discuss any of this with Laurie of course: under the terms of our agreement as I understood it, I had no right to bring anything 'Lewis' to Laurie. Korine in-the-world was a Lewis problem and for Lewis to deal with. In the end, I decided to drop by the cafe on my way home from the library. This meant preparing for a range of eventualities: he might not show up at all. In which case, I asked myself if I was ready to call on him at the Aldersgate Street flat. Was he still in there? No evidence to the contrary. If he did show up at the cafe, he might deflect or lie about any objectives he might have, believing that blindsiding me would give him the advantage down the line. I understood he would likely be late: those who knew him expected him to be up to an hour late. I was ready to wait all afternoon if need be. I'd continue working through *As If*: what I'd read in the library had struck me as of fair to middling quality. I hoped it would pick up.

When I walked through the door, Korine was already seated at a table with direct view of my regular spot. I sat down pretending I hadn't seen him. I waved at Ludo. 'The usual? Coming up!' While I waited for my food to arrive, I busied myself with the novel. Head in it, I didn't read a word. I had yet to decide if and at what point I would make contact with Korine. I was tending towards no and not ever, when he beat me to it. Suddenly, he stood in front of me, plate in hand, and invited himself to join me at my table. He acted as if he wasn't, but I could tell he was nervous. He was also so *there*, I didn't know how else to put it: I resented the power he had over me and what felt like over space itself.

When he said about the role, Cyril, him having landed it, I laughed so loud, for so long. Ludo came over to ask, is everything alright? More than, I replied. Ludo, make yourself scarce, if you don't mind. Me and my friend, we're in the middle of something. 'Good luck with it, Korine,' I said something to the extent of it. 'You do you. I mean, me.' Personally, I had bigger fish to fry. Like pick up my child from his playdate. What time was it, that late already. I winked at Korine as I got up, something I wasn't in the habit of doing. Then I left.

The relief was immense. If I understood anything, it was the mindset and reality of a working actor. On that basis, I was satisfied that the more committed Korine was to his new profession, the more invested in the role, the less likely he was to come for the life I had come to consider my own. On a practical level, he'd have neither the headspace nor the time for anything other than his preparations for the imminent shoot.

I was confronted with the practicalities of recent developments when, days later, the email arrived from my agent. Contract attached, it said. Please sign electronically and return. I ignored it, thinking not my circus, not my monkeys. My agent started calling me. I didn't pick up. She never left a message: I recalled having deactivated the voicemail function a long time ago. I considered getting rid of my phone entirely, drawing a line under the entire affair, I mean, Aubrey Lewis, when I realised that I couldn't. Whatever uneasy truce Korine and I had settled for would be jeopardised if he lost the role. If I didn't cooperate or, worse, if I blocked his endeavours, he would find himself at a loose end, with plenty of opportunity to re-evaluate his decisions. He might look to manage the professional disappointment through the comfort of the familiar, literally. I would be back where I started, practically waiting for him to return and reclaim his life. If I wanted to keep him at arm's length, I had to enable him. Support his ambitions. So I did what I had to: I responded to my agent. I kept my email brief. I signed the contract using my own name, Aubrey Lewis, please find attached. That should do it, I thought. That should keep things ticking along. If I had any reservations about Korine's acting abilities or the lack thereof; if I was at all irritated at the thought of him trading on my name and reputation, and technically, appearing as myself; if I registered that him working under my name would effectively block me from seeking any professional engagements if I needed to for the foreseeable; if I had, was, or did any of these things, I accepted they were the cost of keeping Korine at bay and on that basis worth it.

When Laurie came home that afternoon after an overnight stay – where, she didn't say – I sat at the table in the living room. Cyril was upstairs with a friend he currently despised, direct quote. I had just sent the email to my agent and had lost track of time completely.

'Where are they,' Laurie asked, scanning the room. She looked tired. She wore the same clothes as yesterday: creased, as if she had travelled.

'Come again?'

'Warm as it gets and he's in his in-between-seasons shoes.'

I forgot. I had promised to replace Cyril's sandals.

'One thing's for certain,' Laurie said after a while. 'You're getting better at Korine.'

I made it to the shoe shop just before closing.

As June turned into July, the leaves were dying on account of the unseasonal rain. As I endeavoured to keep on top of my obligations at home, Laurie's throwaway comment, her backhanded compliment, unsettled me on more than one level. On the surface of course, Laurie was affirming me in my role: you're getting better at Korine. But by openly referring to Korine as a third party, she was effectively undermining me in it. She had as good as announced to hypothetical theatregoers that someone, I, was acting while the play was in progress, disrupting the fictive reality. None of it made me feel very secure: if I wasn't Korine, who was I to these people, Laurie and Cyril. A stranger. A stand-in. An arrangement of convenience. I might have a certain use value, but I was not the real deal. If I hadn't already known just how much my sense of safety was tied up with a seemingly arbitrary set of rules that were arrived at when first I entered the household and, by extension, with everybody's compliance with those rules, I did now.

One evening, I sat on the balcony as I often did then. Our child was in the garden, batting away invisible things with a stick. I noticed he was limping again.

'Cyril! Come here,' I called.

'Kirstie,' Laurie called from the living room. How many times. The child's name was Kirstie, not Cyril. She didn't know where I'd got Cyril from.

'Kirstie,' I replied, 'got it.' A boy called Kirstie, I don't see why not. Apparently, it had been Korine's idea.

Looking at the child, now waiting next to me on the balcony, I realised that the strap, that's the strap on his replacement pair of sandals, had torn yet again. On closer inspection, it looked like it had been cut. How was this possible. Someone did that? He'd have to have taken the sandal off in the first place? Laurie, who'd joined us outside, first mooted the possibility that he was being bullied at school. It shifted the tenor of the conversation. We sat him down and tried talking to him. He wouldn't say. Instead, he started on Mallorca again. How he wished that his real parents would come, rescue him from us and take him on holiday. A real holiday, not Bognor Regis. He hated Bognor Regis. Hated us. Just something children say, Laurie assured me, and yet, the real-parent comment stung.

Next day on the school run, in a marked departure from my routine, I went up to every parent waiting by the gate and showed them the sandal. The evidence, I called it. Did their child have a problem with my child? Their child, any priors? Behavioural issues? This little innocent-looking thing with the glasses on a strap – any routine suspensions from school? Suspect habits? I didn't get anywhere. The gathered parents took a collective step backwards, so to speak. That moment Kirstie came out of the building, carrying his satchel. Seeing what I was doing, embarrassing him, he started to cry. It felt as if a sinkhole opened where I stood: I didn't even know how to pretend to be a parent. I was doing it wrong. I took my child by the hand and dragged him to the old-fashioned travel agency on Whitecross

Street. Assisted by one Mrs Syed, I booked a package holiday to Mallorca, all inclusive, spending over half of what was left of my savings. Kirstie's little face when I let him carry the flight tickets home: so bright, so happy.

7

'And scene!' Howe called. Circa forty of us – director, actors, producers, first and second assistant directors, and others whose place cards contained unfamiliar jargon – sat around a U-shaped arrangement of tables. Glasses of water and dog-eared, heavily marked-up copies of the script in front of us. Seconds passed in which nobody moved. Nobody made a sound. More people, crew members, I didn't know who, were lined up against the walls of the room, balancing copies of the script on their knees. They, too, were entirely silent. Everyone waited for someone else to pass verdict first.

I came round to all this. Did it happen? How did I do? Was I too subtle, or did I overact? What did I do with my arms and legs? I hadn't waved, had I? I'd promised myself to not wave, to repress any instinct to wave I might have. All I could say with certainty was that, in that final scene and the build-up to it, I had felt my character's, Cyril's, sadness. I'd not felt this sad for a long while, not as Korine, I mean, Lewis. But during the read-through, sitting at the head of the U-shaped table arrangement in an uninspiring conference room at the back of a large studio complex northwest of London, I felt dejected. It made me think: where did this come from. What resources was I tapping into. While I was acting, I had wondered whether, now that the sadness had started, it would ever stop. Would it overtake my regular life. But it started to recede as soon as I heard Howe call the scene. It was dying away still as I tried to get a handle on the situation.

My co-lead, Drew Atkins, who sat next to me on my left, made the first move. She turned to look at me and gave me an underplayed smile. I reciprocated and, finally, the tension broke: Howe started clapping as if she meant it. It seemed as though she were clapping for me specifically. I did that thing where you turn around to check the applause wasn't meant for somebody else: no one behind me. Then the entire room followed suit: hollering, whooping. The noise grew and extended to include everyone in and outside of the room who'd helped us get to this point. Consensus was, the cast gelled.

Afterwards, actors and crew gathered in front of a long table at the far wall of the room. Refreshments had been laid out, nothing fancy, sandwiches in cling film, that sort of thing. I stood in the corner, a head taller than anyone, holding a paper plate: something damp on it made it lose integrity fast. I felt awkward. Everyone seemed to know everyone else. Too nervous to eat, I focused on my Oslos which had come out of retirement for the occasion. I tried smiling at no one in particular, conveying an ambient sort of conviviality, not something that had worked for me historically. I was surprised when Atkins came up to me.

'Aubrey Lewis,' she said. 'Sight for sore eyes.'

'You too,' I said ineptly.

'I'm sorry about Laurie,' she said. She appeared to mean it.

'What can you do.' I thought of Laurie my wife rather than Lewis's, which I felt gave me a convincing air of regret.

'I tried to call,' Atkins said.

I didn't know how to respond. Tried? Did she or didn't she call? When? Was she suggesting that I, Lewis, had failed to return her calls? The extent of her familiarity, her awareness of Lewis's personal circumstances, caught me unaware. 'How is the husband?' I said, finally, for something to say.

'Wife,' Atkins corrected me after a pause. 'Lewis . . . *wife*.'

I realised then that I had a problem. That this was the part I had failed to prepare for. In the run-up to the read-through, I had been so preoccupied with my ability to read fluently and stay on script that I had failed to consider relationship histories between actors and crew. Any remaining emotional energy had been devoted to a secondary fear that Lewis might turn up and oust me at the last minute. While I had expected and been looking forward to meeting D. Smiff, Smith's wife from *People*, restyled as Darryl in *As If*, I had neglected to consider that the actor who played her, Drew Atkins, knew Lewis in real life. Christ, they had worked together for years. Come to think of it: hadn't he mentioned her that first night in the flat? Called her a friend? I was unable to imagine Lewis in an extended social field, was my excuse. I struggled to imagine him as anything other than apart from the crowd: a tactical blunder as it turned out.

Howe came over as if to the rescue. 'Aubrey! Drew! Thanks for today.' Pivoting towards me: 'You did it, Aubrey.' Towards Atkins: 'What did I tell you. He's back.'

Atkins kept quiet. Gave a hesitant smile.

If Howe detected the tension between us, she didn't say. She was here to talk about the imminent shoot: the director and writers would make some final changes to the script in response to what we the actors had brought to the table in terms of character subtleties, she said. Expect a courier on Saturday night, or Sunday morning, to deliver the latest. God! So much to do still.

Amen to that. As I stood there, paper plate in hand, the immensity of the task ahead started to dawn on me. Playing the part of Cyril was one thing. The difference between me and the other actors on set was that my performance would have to continue in between takes: I had to be Aubrey Lewis, and credibly so. I had to know who he knew, in what capacity. Who he had collaborated with in the past, on *People* and other productions. That supporting actor – older woman – who'd accosted me by the buffet earlier, big smile, big personality: who was she to me. The person currently trying to catch my eye from across the room: did we have history? Slowly I was becoming aware that every move I made or did not make had the potential to alienate natural allies.

Towards the end of the social, one of the runners put me in a car with a chauffeur: the latter would drop me off at the flat and continue to take me back and forth every day for the length of the shoot. Lead actor privilege, I understood. (I myself used to work as a chauffeur for a private car hire company twenty-ten to -eleven: the money was decent, but ultimately, it wasn't for me.) As soon as I got out on Aldersgate Street, I raced up the stairs, three four steps at a time. Once inside, I made a quick sandwich involving two slices of processed cheese which I ate standing up at the sink. Then I lay back on the sofa, knees pulled up, and opened Lewis's laptop. There would be no resting on any laurels. No taking a moment to acknowledge how far I had come. Ahead of the first day of shooting, this coming Tuesday, I would compile an in-depth lexicon, a who's who of *As If*, the production, to help me navigate the set. The real work started now.

I began by making a preliminary list of, first, my scene partners, then every actor involved in the production. I matched faces to names relatively quickly. I proceeded to trail through online databases, old reviews and interviews to establish potential overlaps in lists of appearances. I scoured social media, too: theirs, not Lewis's. Other than a few largely dormant fan accounts – one-point-five-k followers on Instagram sort of thing – he didn't have any. The research was hard going, not helped by paywalls nor my lack of digital literacy: I didn't have clever ways of bypassing anything. Not for the first time did I regret having only half listened when Lewis had shared his life story that first night. In fact, I wished he was here to tell it again: he'd have the gossip beyond the internet factoids. Failing that, I resorted to watching programmes he'd been in on various streaming platforms, primarily YouTube and iPlayer. I rewatched a dozen or so episodes of *People*: that guy playing Smythe, Clemens something? I'd seen him outside the studio earlier, arguing on the phone. I recognised the actor who played Smith, too. He'd left early. In hindsight, I'd say I was focusing more on Lewis's ways of approaching his role – how he employed certain mannerisms and gestures to indicate a change in mood e.g. – rather than on the all-important behind-the-scenes info.

On Sunday morning the revised script came via a courier. I was in a rabbit hole online, fifteen names on the list (of sixty) tracked and identified. I was acutely aware that, apart from Howe, I hadn't even thought of crew members yet. I put the script on the floor where, over the subsequent thirty-six hours, it got buried under a mounting pile of A4 sheets of paper covered in notes. I forgot about it until Monday night (!) when I realised the changes were relatively extensive.

The car collected me on Tuesday the second of July at five in the morning. First thing on arrival, I met Atkins in the studio canteen queuing for coffee. I was pleased to make reference to her *Mother Courage* at the Royal Court, as well as a trip we'd made to the Côte d'Azur in two-thousand-seven with our wives. 'Break a leg, Lewis,' Atkins said, smiling. 'You, too,' I replied. So far, so good.

It went downhill from there. Fourth or fifth person I encountered on set, I offended. I was sitting in make-up for the first time when the mood dropped for no fault of my own. Apparently — and I gathered this from the third assistant director, who managed the subsequent complaint and who pulled me aside to have a word later that day — I slighted Nancy P. the make-up artist who I'd bonded with during a shoot in Basildon, Essex, some years ago. I failed to reciprocate friendly signs of recognition, rude, then did not respond to her comments about some eyelid, *my* eyelid, I gathered, implicitly casting doubt over or not affirming her version of events, technically gaslighting her. I didn't treat her like a respected colleague but reduced her to a service provider, which got her back up. She had worked in make-up for thirty years if she counted her internship – big stars, A-listers – and never had anyone and so on and so forth. The third assistant director said to apologise. To deal with the matter head-on before relations deteriorated further. I promised I would. I intended to.

Day one went from bad to worse. Already the read-through had brought with it unfamiliar jargon, like first, second and third assistant director, I mean, how many of them were there. But the extent of my lack of professionalism didn't hit home until I set foot on the set. In terms of directives, I knew 'action', 'scene' and 'cut', but what else. Dirty shot, quiet on set. Last looks! which seemed to draw Nancy out. Camera right, I walked right rather than left from my point of view. I was asked to 'cheat a bit', I hadn't a clue. Howe kept walking up to me, taking me by the shoulders and physically manoeuvring me into position: it was embarrassing. Roll rehearsing the shot was clear enough. 'Mark it!' I thought meant action, it was voiced with a similar urgency. But when I started acting the scene, I ended up walking straight into the clapper operator trying, I got it, to mark the shot. On one particularly regretful occasion, in response to yet another counterintuitive directive, I stopped acting completely. I came out of character before Howe called cut. My scene partners sniggered, apart from one who blushed vicariously. The crew looked horrified. 'Cut!' Howe called after the event. 'Cut.' Seconds passed before she managed to smile at me reassuringly. 'Out of practice,' I overheard her say to the second assistant director. 'He'll get into the swing of it.' To the room: 'Ok, going again!'

By the end of the day, my confidence was on the floor. I had to contend with the fact that the job had yet another layer to it: I had to appear as if I were an experienced actor. As if that weren't enough, my portrayal of an experienced actor had to convince a large number of experienced actors and crew on set. In short, I had to feign knowhow. How was that different from acquiring it, it probably wasn't. That night, I perused countless online resources: 'Filmmaking' on Wikipedia e.g., and 'Film Set Etiquette: Nine Things You Should Never Do'. I went through the comments on various actors' forums trying to pick up the lingo. I searched, how does TV work, well, work. I didn't get to rehearsing my actual lines until the following morning, in the car on the M4. Strange as it may seem, at no point did I consider giving up. On the contrary: I was acutely aware I was living the dream.

Day two was better. Day three, so so. Day four consisted of a series of gaffes: I was so focused on the practicalities of being an actor that I forgot to act. I responded to directives more reliably and at times enthusiastically, but my performance fell flat. Howe kept insisting I 'get in the zone' which made matters worse: I no longer knew whether I was coming or going and it showed: I had an expressive face, had not learnt to emotionally regulate. I'd not felt the need to until recently.

At the end of the day, Howe and Atkins intercepted me on my way out. I feared the worst.

'What are you up to,' Howe asked. 'Do you want to find a quiet corner and run through some of tomorrow's scenes together?'

'What, now? Don't you have places to go?'

'What, and miss this?' Atkins said.

'Places, what places' – Howe.

I let them lead me through the deserted studio, past the few remaining technicians dismantling the set and a cleaner pushing a cart. We soon found an empty changing room near Stage 3: a typical set-up with lockers, wooden benches, racks with hooks and a water dispenser. Howe and Atkins sat down on opposite benches, the former directing me to sit next to the latter. Before I knew it, Atkins turned to me and shook me by the shoulders.

'Relax, Lewis. Acting is just pretending, remember?'

Without warning, she started on a tense scene, an argument, scheduled to be shot in the morning. She was talking in character too close to my face. I recoiled.

'Lewis, stay with it. Do Cyril. Got your lines?'

I did. I thought I did.

'Listen to Atkins, I mean Darryl. React.'

And react I did: after a dozen takes, I managed to reciprocate Atkins's intensity. I defended, got angry, as Cyril. Take thirty, Howe started paying attention. She sat up and pretended to film us through a viewfinder she shaped with her hands. Another couple of takes, and she got out her phone and started filming for real. Eventually, we landed on a version that prompted Howe to drop her phone in her lap and raise her arms as if to say what did I tell you! That wasn't so hard, was it! Now, how did I do that again, I said. No way could I repeat the performance. Then I did. Twice. At this point, Atkins started clapping, grinning: she meant it, I could tell. 'There he is,' Howe said, 'Aubrey Lewis as he lives and breathes.' As a response, I leapt onto one of the benches and, unprompted, delivered my audition monologue, nailing it in one.

It got better after that. Day five earned me a round of applause from the crew when I followed a particular directorial cue I'd been missing – back to firsts – correctly for once. Day eight saw me coax an extra into delivering, and I quote, the improv of her life. By day ten the tide really was turning: I was starting to gain, if not respect, then acceptance from my colleagues. They started treating me with civility. With how-was-your-weekend sort of basic geniality. Fancy a Coke? Packet of chewing gum going round: want one? Normal exchanges. Courtesies.

The headline was, I was doing it. I was surviving on a professional set. Deprofessionalising it by default, but nevertheless.

Four weeks into the shoot, I lost the flat. On the

evening of the first of August, I tried to get in and found that the front door was locked. When I knocked, calling 'hello!' repeatedly, a stranger opened. 'Can I help?' he said. He did not take me for Lewis, from which I concluded they'd not met in person. 'I live here,' I said. 'No you don't,' the stranger replied. He explained that his subtenant had decided to cancel his contract with minimal notice which inconvenienced him greatly. Not only that, but the subtenant in question had failed to remove his possessions. Now, who was I. Was I him? No, I said. I was Lindsey Korine. The name meant nothing to him. Now that I was here: did I want to take anything. He'd arranged for cleaning professionals to clear out the flat in the morning. If I wanted anything, I should collect it now. To think I had taken exception to the flat when first I arrived: how I'd hated the hard-plastic chairs, their cracked, somewhat sinister shade of red. How I'd railed against the nonoperational radiators: it would be a wrench to leave them for good. The sublessor said he did not have all day. I went in and saved what I could. I'd not worn a jacket or coat since June, but with the autumn incoming, I went straight for the old favourites: the tweed and wax items which had found their way back to the stand. I took *As If*, the original novel. I carried what little cash was left around with me anyway. I left the who's who I never finished behind (stashes of A4 paper) and, regrettably, the laptop. Was I done? the sublessor asked. If I wouldn't mind, he'd like to get back to recording his TikTok whatever. When I was halfway down the stairs, I heard the key turn in the lock.

If anyone noticed the double layers I was wearing to work the next day, they didn't say. I got through the day as well as might be expected. By the end of it, after exchanging the usual see-you-tomorrows with the cast and crew, I went out to my pick-up spot to tell the driver that I wouldn't be needing her services for the foreseeable. Then I returned inside. Unaccosted, I made my way towards the changing room near Stage 3, the one with the lockers. It was as spacious as I remembered. Warm, too. There were sinks, showers and toilets in the back which would serve me well. I proceeded to lay out my tweed coat on what I thought of as Howe's bench, devising a provisional bed.

For a while, I got away with it: in the morning I would get up, gather together my possessions – my coat-mattress, my wax-jacket-pillow – and store them in one of the lockers. I would wash superficially and brush my teeth, preferably in the second sink from the left. Once I'd made sure I'd removed any evidence of my presence, I'd slip out of the changing room. I would wander the corridors for a while, visit the cafeteria, then turn up on set, frequently early. Two nights became three, then four. No incidents until my fifth evening in the changing room: I was practising a difficult scene scheduled to be shot the next day not as subdued as I should have, when the second assistant director walked in on me. I must've made for a strange sight in my vest and trousers. The radio was blaring through the pay-as-you-go phone I'd invested in and a paper plate filled with leftover goulash was balancing between sinks. 'Everything ok in here? Aubrey?' The second assistant director took in the rare version of domesticity that presented itself for several overlong seconds, before turning around and walking out. From then on, I was on borrowed time.

My biggest regret? My popularity on set plateaued, then deteriorated again: not helped by emerging rumours around my housing situation, nor, I suspected, Nancy P.'s machinations. Five weeks into the shoot, I had yet to apologise to the make-up artist. It mightn't have made any difference: I'd found out that she had it in for Lewis. Some beef in the past. What I hadn't reckoned with was the extent to which she went out of her way to spread discontent: she was actively turning colleagues against me. I had no evidence of this, other than the fact that some members of the crew and several actors started treating me with renewed reserve. They would hang in a small group, and when I joined, they disbanded. Things to see to, all of a sudden. Duty calls, slap on the back. When I told Howe, she said not to worry. As the lead actor, I would attract this sort of resentment. It came with the territory. It would serve me well to remember my privilege. I found it hard to get my head around this.

But the worst was the talking behind my back. Specifically, there was talk that I wasn't the same Lewis. Like, nowhere near. Who was this guy. Who was the chaos agent. The wax jacket, did you smell it. Who are you and what have you done with Aubrey Lewis. In many ways, my worst fears were confirmed: I wasn't doing it right, 'it' meaning Lewis. Whatever I'd done and continued to do to portray him as accurately as I could, it was evident that I failed to convince: the cast and crew weren't buying it. It came to a head when one of the other actors,

Clemens, called me out in front of everyone after a scene gone bad. I ended up walking off set. Once I'd calmed down, I conceded I might have overreacted. I might have read too much into his remark. The third assistant director, who'd been sent after me to manage me, said that I had. What Clemens had said: 'Who does he think he is?' How did a casual remark justify a tantrum, the third assistant director didn't get it.

Either the second assistant director finally talked, or they happened across me during a routine inspection: in the early morning of my twelfth night in the changing room, security caught me in the act, that is, wrapped in my tweed coat, asleep on one of the wooden benches. They cleared me out with immediate effect. If Howe was informed, and I believe that she wasn't, she didn't mention it. I thought about confiding in her or Atkins, asking them for help, and I almost did on a couple of occasions, but, on top of their own familial and professional responsibilities, neither of them had the capacity to babysit me. And why should they. If I couldn't take care of others, if I'd proven that was the case, the least I could do was take care of myself. I told the driver I would be needing her services again. That night, I returned to

Clerkenwell, the area I'd lived in for the last thirty years. It looked like it might rain, so I retreated to the Barbican underpass. As soon as I settled down on the pavement, I started thinking of Lewis: I didn't harbour any resentments towards him for failing to renew the contract of the flat, nor for retaining my fee, the first instalment of which should've cleared in his account by now. I wasn't in it for the flat nor the money. I'd never been in anything for the compensation: to my detriment, Laurie would say. If anything, I felt that *I* owed *him*. I owed him everything. In fact, I didn't half hope I would see him again: that one day, he would walk past me in his tracksuit like he did when I was at my lowest that night many weeks ago. I would go after him and tell him: thank him, even. Failing that, I would talk to him in his absence, or I should say: a romanticised version of him. Preparing the following day's performance, I might ask him which interpretation he preferred, this way or another. Should I pronounce the vowel there 'ah' or 'e'. What, in his opinion, was Cyril's intent in this particular scenelet: what does he want, what does he think he wants and how unbridgeable is the difference. What is he chasing, at the expense of what else. How much of a fool does he end up making of himself et cetera. In my head, Lewis's responses were universally benign and supportive.

Every morning, I'd wait on Aldersgate Street for the car to pick me up. Lead actor privilege, lest I forget.

If an indication was needed as to the extent to which I was failing to go anywhere near the loss of my family, here it was: one August evening, en route to the underpass, I saw Lewis from a distance, my family in tow. Shell-shocked, I looked right past my wife and child and fixated on Lewis: the logical extension of the coping strategy I'd been employing over the last three months. He was no longer wearing his tracksuit, but something along the lines of Jelley's clothes. Unless it was Jelley. I didn't think it was. I hid between two buildings thinking if he saw me he might turn the other way: an instinct which threw the perfectly mutual relationship I'd built up in my head into relief. When he – they – passed me at close distance, I pressed myself against the wall as flat as possible. Lewis was laughing at something my child said. Hearing Kirstie's voice, I thought I'd pass out. I decided there and then that I couldn't lose track of them, I mean, him: in fact, I latched on to the idea that Lewis was the answer to at least one of my problems. The more time I could spend in his presence, observing him – his movements, his mannerisms – the more convincingly I would be able to play him on set. My Lewis would shut up my critics and anyone who'd been badmouthing me professionally. I would avoid social death on set: this was what I believed – what I convinced myself – was at stake. I followed them into Fann Street at a safe distance, then left up Golden Lane. It wasn't as if I didn't know where they were going: past Stanley Cohen House and into the familiar entrance block to Basterfield House. Lewis appeared to have the code that released the lock electronically.

Once the family had disappeared inside, I went round the back towards the communal garden. I positioned myself at the far edge of it, close to Bayer House, from where I could survey the entire facade of Basterfield House without running the risk of being seen myself. I discerned general movement in their flat, a choreography of sorts. Pretty to watch, but of no particular use value. An hour in, I realised that half the time I'd been watching the neighbouring flat by mistake. It wouldn't do. I moved further into the communal garden, I had to. Specifically, I hid behind the isolated conifer, a deodar cedar, according to Laurie, at the centre of it: from here, I had a direct view of their living room. I watched Lewis unwrap a sandwich for Kirstie, handing it to him while talking. How he laughed when the child dropped it onto the floor within seconds. He proceeded to dust it off and eat it himself. I started to register an unpleasant, unnamed feeling building in me and redoubled my focus on the task at hand. I copied Lewis's movements in real time: no, not like that. Again. Better. Again. Better still. I patted air the height of my hip like he patted the child's head. Gently. Lanky arm, loose in the elbow. So engrossed was I, watching, practising, already improving and getting the detail right, that I forgot where I was, drawing unwanted attention to myself: he must've seen something, for he stopped what he was doing and turned in my direction. He came out onto the balcony, scanning the garden. He yelled, then went back inside. A minute later, he returned with a – my – camping chair and parked himself near the railing. This was how he did anger, I noted. Fear, stubbornness, in there too. It was fascinating: a wealth of material I could put to good use. I waited until dusk, then left unseen.

I decided to spend the night in the entrance block

of Basterfield House, staying close to my research subject. Slipping in behind someone in possession of the latest access code, easy enough. I proceeded to sit down sideways on a step in the upper third of the first flight of stairs, feet propped against the banister, back against the cold wall, clamping myself into position. Over the subsequent several hours, I overheard conversations in passing: residents, visitors, delivery people. No one seemed to recognise me, such was the extent to which I presented out of context: why would Lindsey Korine of number sixteen sit in the entrance block, it didn't compute. It wasn't like they overlooked me completely: how could they, my position slowed everyone down. People would stand in front of me, requesting I get out of the way. When I showed no sign of moving, they tended to climb over me, complaining, or back off and take the lift. This led to often disturbing insights into human behaviour. I fell into a depressive register as a result, or else because of the disconnect I was labouring in vain to maintain.

A bad night was followed by a worse day on set. For the first time since shooting began over six weeks ago, I didn't want to be there. I got it in my head that I wasn't ready. That my time would be better spent studying Lewis. The longer I had with him now, the fewer problems I would have in the long run. But the hard truth was this: where it was painful to see him with my wife and child, knowing they were together and not seeing them felt even worse. On set, I spent the day lying low between scenes, avoiding people. A security guard had been installed at the door to the changing room, I did check, so I sat in a corridor, away from the action. When I saw Atkins approach, I hid my face in my hands like a child wishing not to be seen.

'Lewis? What are you doing.'

'What's it look like.' I reluctantly dropped my hands to look up at her.

'I don't know, love. What *does* it look like, you tell me.'

'I'll just sit here if you don't mind.'

'You do you, Lewis,' she said after a while, looking concerned. She left me to it, but within half an hour, one of the special effects team came to fetch me, insisting I sit in his workshop for a while. Atkins had sent him. Some company, do me good. I got through the rest of the day watching him build a rain machine, counting the minutes.

As soon as the car dropped me off on Aldersgate

Street, I made for Basterfield House. Suddenly I felt animated. That's the low-energy-expenditure day paying, I thought. I'd already decided that my previous vantage point, while acceptable, could be improved on. One of the architectural idiosyncrasies of Basterfield House: sets of concrete steps provided direct access from the communal garden to the balconies of the upper-ground-floor maisonettes. My former home, my destination. I pushed my way through the herbaceous perennials, the reeds, the tall yucca and the Judas tree that, among other exotic vegetation, bordered the garden, until I arrived at the flat. Ducking, I mounted the steps which led to the balcony. On it, I went down on my hands and knees, making directly for the corner under the right-hand window – the one part of the frontage that wasn't transparent, panelled from waist-height down, and capable of facilitating a person in hiding. It was worth it: if I popped up my head I had a clear view of the living room, them in it, and into the kitchen. Through the single-glazed windows, I could hear their conversation. Lewis was saying something that Laurie found entertaining. Had the child in stitches, too. I was so caught up in the scene that I joined in with the laughter, quietly, privately, pressing myself against the panel that separated me from them, its mad yet reassuring maroon. I had to remind myself that this wasn't a jolly. I was here in service of my performance and my performance only. Then, unexpectedly, the tone of the conversation inside the flat changed. Laurie and Lewis were arguing, putting their heads together over what, Kirstie's sandal? I couldn't quite get the detail, but Laurie wanted to inform the head teacher whereas Lewis did not. 'Just leave it,' Lewis kept saying. 'Laurie, just let it rest. It's the summer break.' He looked overwrought. I made a mental note: stern look, gritted teeth. Moving his arms a lot. Hand on forehead. Off it. Hand in hair like a headband. Taking it out again. This was it. I could use this. What else.

I half got up so as to see better, crouching, back bent. Straightening up, I gained another half inch: better still. Laurie was wearing one of the sweatshirts I'd left, advertising *Terrace House* of all things, funny, and without thinking I called her, or something like her name slipped out. I held my mouth shut immediately, panicked, mortified. Laurie hadn't heard, but Lewis had: he turned and our eyes met. He was going to come for me, he had that air about him that preceded violent action. Then Kirstie started crying – whether as a response to the adults' arguing or else my presence, I didn't know. I feared it was the latter. With Lewis temporarily distracted, consoling my child, I rose to my full height, turned around and ran away.

As I left the estate and headed towards the underpass, the perfect normality – the domesticity – of the scene I had witnessed landed with me. Laurie had looked tired but happier, if that wasn't too strong a word, than when last I knew her. Kirstie seemed to relate to Lewis entirely naturally: even the crying was progress, considering he'd shut down completely when Laurie got ill. The family unit functioned, interpersonal tensions and everyday conflicts notwithstanding. If there was a problem, and there was, it was me: if I kept up my pursuit of Lewis, I risked interfering with the life my wife and child were in the process of rebuilding. Who would benefit from my presence? What would it do, other than reopen old wounds. Turning left into Beech Street, I promised myself that this would be the last they'd see of me. The least I could do was let them get on with their lives.

If on set things went south less rapidly than before, if I turned another corner, it was because I was getting better at Lewis. Where I'd failed to convince for the longest time, eventually people began to replace or confuse the Aubrey Lewis they knew with the version I gave them and that they interacted with on a day-to-day basis. Either the scrupulous study of my subject was starting to pay off and I had improved the accuracy with which I portrayed him, or I persuaded on another level: like a good actor might. In other words, I was delivering the sort of performance that asserted itself over the historical subject, it isn't unheard of or even rare: try thinking of the playwright Joe Orton: you get Gary Oldman. Whatever it was, the gossip died down. In fact, people started talking to me again. Moreover, I told Drew Atkins that I had started to grieve the loss of my wife and child. It was a good thing, I said. I took comfort in knowing they were in a better place now. Child, Atkins replied. What child. Never mind, I said. Eventually, even Nancy the make-up artist came round to me. For no discernible reason our relationship moved into a more grown-up register. I guess she didn't want to be left behind as the tide turned in my favour.

But all wasn't well. Where my Lewis improved, my Cyril did not. Where I'd been putting my all into the former, I'd neglected the latter. I was routinely underprepared. I don't just mean I messed up my lines: I showed up barely knowing them. To make matters worse, I physically deteriorated to an extent I couldn't cover up or override: the consequence of the pressure I'd put myself under. The triple workload. The nights in the open air or the Barbican underpass. The reality that I'd irrevocably surrendered my family. I couldn't get through a scene without sighing. I started tic-ing, too: the sort of involuntary movement not just picked up by but accentuated on camera. People wanted me to do well at this point – Howe and Atkins in particular never wavered in their support – but none of it went unnoticed. It came to a head when I missed a script that had been updated at the last minute and couriered to my former address on Aldersgate Street. I had barely retained the original version and I did not find it in me to learn the latest edit on the spot. Controversially, Howe resorted to moving all of my scenes to the latter half of the day, a delay which affected not just my scene partners, but the actors and crew whose scenes were brought forward in lieu. I felt bad. I was concerned about the effects it would have on my newfound acceptance on set. But Howe ordered me to barricade myself into a small office at the back of the production facility and learn my lines. In fact, she walked me there. 'Do you have everything you need? Do you want me to lock the door? Call me if you need anything. Otherwise, get to it, Lewis. We're relying on you.' When we finally came to shooting near the end of the day, I couldn't do it. I was sorry. So sorry, but no. I had nothing.

That night, precisely eight weeks into the shoot, Howe took me to one side. What was going on, she asked. I seemed distracted. Was there anything she could do to support. I told her there wasn't. But a project that had been dragging on my resources lately had run its natural course. I would be able to reprioritise as of now. Concentrate on Kirstie, sorry, Cyril. Cyril and Cyril alone.

It was too late to reprioritise. I had run out of road. Howe didn't want to, but in the end her hand was forced. Enter the understudy, Lucien Jelley. It was as if he'd been hiding in the wings all this time, waiting for me to trip up.

8

I saw Korine on Golden Lane in mid-August. Laurie, Kirstie and I were walking home from a reading challenge organised by the local library, when I noticed him hiding behind a lamp post. He followed us from there. Each time I looked back, there he was, hiding behind every lamp post along the way. No let-up after that: so sure was I later that afternoon that I'd seen eyes in the deodar cedar, the better to see you with, that I dropped what I was doing – talking to Laurie, feeding the child – and charged onto the balcony. 'Korine!' I called. 'Show yourself, coward!' No answer and yet, unnaturally shuddering branches. I went back inside, circling the room, scaring the child. 'What are you doing,' Laurie asked. 'What does it look like,' I replied. I fetched the camping chair from the built-in wardrobe in the hall and went on to install myself in front of the balcony door. I'd stay out here tonight, I informed Laurie. Somebody had to. 'Come on, Kirstie,' she said. 'Let's go upstairs. Let's remove ourselves from whatever this is.' At circa ten p.m. she came out to bring me my jean jacket. Did I want it. The evenings were getting cooler. Christmas in the air already oh dear. I politely declined. I needed elbow room to react quicker in the eventuality.

I was aware of the risk I'd taken making Korine homeless. It went against my declared aim to enable him and in that sense against my better judgement. And yet I'd cancelled the flat on Aldersgate Street effective the first of August and redirected the money I saved towards Laurie. I'd seen no other way: my outgoings were up and my savings were dwindling dramatically. Even if I'd found it in me, I couldn't get in touch with my agent to ask her to put me forward for jobs while *As If* was still being filmed and 'I', Korine, already engaged. So I unenthusiastically started applying for work through the local job centre. Not once did I make it as far as the interview stage. I would have thought I'd acquired transferable skills as an actor, but it seemed that I lacked the relevant experience for every kind of remunerative employment. Not even my job in the sports shop thirty years ago counted for anything: everything was so different now (in 'digital'). At forty-six I was seen to be past it, incapable of acquiring new skills. That's what I told Laurie anyway. Honestly, I didn't try very hard. How could I go to work. Who'd pick up Kirstie from his various summer activities. Who'd look after him while Laurie was out. This wasn't about his behaviour which, while on the subject, had been deteriorating. One afternoon, we're talking the end of July, I had found an automatic knife, spring-activated, under his mattress. I didn't even know what it was at first. It clunked to the floor when I changed the sheets: thick, heavy, like a six-inch club. When I investigated, I found a switch near the top of what I now know was the handle: I pushed it and – Christ! – a steel blade shot out the front. I hectically worked out how to retract it, calling the boy: 'Kirstie! Come up here *instantly*!' Seconds later, he stood in the door frame. He turned white when he saw the knife. 'What is this.' I proffered the weapon. He started to cry. 'Where did you get this from?' He cried even harder. Eventually, I got him to admit to employing a chair to fetch the knife from the top shelf of his parents' wardrobe. He didn't know whether it belonged to his mum or his dad. (He said 'dad', meaning Korine.) 'Why did you take it,' I asked. He didn't say but looked down at his socked feet. That's when it dawned on me: what if he had been cutting the straps of his own sandals in a last-ditch attempt at manoeuvring himself nearer the centre of a world that had been sidelining him? As I went down on my knees to hug him, potentially reinforcing his desperate behaviour, the phrase epic parental failure went through my head and I included myself. I confiscated the weapon and promised that I wouldn't tell Laurie. 'Go on,' I said, 'you can go now. It's fine. It'll be fine.' What was an out-the-front automatic knife doing in the flat, was what I really wanted to know. Who owned such a thing. There were further signs that all wasn't well: Kirstie routinely declaring he detested his clothes, all of them. He detested his monkey. (Called it 'chubby', all of a sudden. Where did that come from.) He repeatedly brought up a kitten that, barely received, had been taken from him. And when when when would we go to Mallorca. All of his friends were away over the summer break: at their parents' country houses or abroad. Why did he have to wait until September. It wasn't fair. Laurie said he was picking up on my stress levels and the recent tensions between us. Be that as it may, leaving the child unsupervised for hours on end while I was at work or entering whatever data into databases remotely was out of the question. I couldn't do it, not with everything going on.

Certainly not with Korine at large. I began to have kidnapping fantasies: Korine taking Kirstie by the hand while I wasn't looking, the latter not resisting or crying for help but following him unquestioningly, unaware that a fateful exchange had taken place. Or, worse, aware of it and not caring. I don't know why I went there: I'd disabused myself of the notion that Korine was a man with regrets, trying to get his family back. If he wanted to, he could have contacted Laurie a long time ago: there was nothing stopping him from going behind my back, sweet-talking her into allowing him in. In truth, and I should've known this, Korine wasn't after his wife nor child. He was after me. Always had been. Why else target me months ago? Infiltrate my flat, my supposed safe space? Question was, what did he want from me. Who, for that matter, did I mean by 'me'—

Laurie continued to breach and eventually change the rules of engagement as I knew them. For starters, she took to calling me by my actual name which I'd volunteered when we first met: Aubrey this, Aubrey that. No more Lindsey. And she built on the quip about getting good at Korine and made a habit of talking about him in the third person. The morning after I'd spotted Korine on Golden Lane, Laurie and I were sitting on the balcony discussing the deodar cedar in the garden. I thought it withered. She thought it waterlogged. Out of nowhere a one-eyed kitten appeared, parading along the balcony railing, left to right. Once it reached the end, it leapt down and into the grass. It vanished from sight before reappearing again: it tore up the cedar and sat on top like a deranged Christmas angel, snarling at nothing. The kitten had been roaming the estate, Laurie said, for weeks now. She took this as an excuse to start telling me about Korine: there, his name again, referring to him rather than myself: little things: little digs, constantly. Lindsey loved Christmas, Laurie said. But he had a problem with cats. He was always reading, anything he could get his hands on. He was smart, but he lacked the ambition to make anything out of himself. Something to do with his father – Laurie wasn't a psychologist – or wider working-class cultures of refusal – she wasn't a cultural theorist. As a consequence, he was forever quitting menial jobs. The latest casualty: data entry. He hadn't coped with her illness either, Laurie continued. Or actually, he'd held it together while it was all going on, then fallen apart at the end of it. Typically, he had refused to seek help. This was the final straw for her. It wasn't like she didn't love him, but he was a liability. They'd married too young, she said, almost apologetically.

Laurie telling me about Korine, her husband, should've reassured me: not only did she trust me enough to confide in me, but she was telling me in no uncertain terms that she didn't believe that they, Korine and herself, could come back from where they had left things. She was letting me know that, despite the compromises involved, the current arrangement was preferable to having him back. And yet, my anxiety levels went through the roof. Changing the way she addressed me, routinely referring to Korine in the third person, Laurie wasn't just undermining me in my role. She was undermining and incrementally eroding the role itself. The pretence was no longer needed, Laurie seemed to suggest. We'd done a thing and now we no longer had to. You wouldn't continue wearing inflatable armbands either, once you could swim. I realised then it was acting itself I'd got invested in. Over the last eleven, twelve weeks, the daily act of performing Korine had become as important to me as participating in family life, our version of it. I didn't know what that said about me. Whether I was as selfish as Korine. But lately, I'd been doing what I did best: acting: disappearing into a role. Playing Korine, I felt more like myself than I had in years. I felt my internal spring tightening and, while it scared me, I also liked it.

That same evening, I saw him on, that is *on*, our balcony. Laurie and I were arguing, when I heard someone call out her name. I looked up and saw Korine's head in the leftmost window, hands in front of his mouth. The audacity. The complete lack of restraint. This was the furthest he'd dared to encroach so far. Luckily Laurie hadn't heard. She was facing my way, that is, away from the window. Korine didn't move. For a moment, he looked like he might get up, take the camping chair by its backrest, smash in the glass frontage and enter the flat. He had that air about him, the sort of air that precedes violent action. What would I do, confronted with the reality of him? How would I protect myself and my family? At this point, I noticed that Kirstie had started to cry, expressing what I for one felt. By the time I turned back to Korine, he was hurtling down the steps that led into the garden. He ran past the deodar cedar and, turning left, out of the estate. Preferable to him going on the offensive, and yet I considered his behaviour an escalation. A clear provocation. A declaration of war. The man was emboldened: no way of knowing what he would do next.

Adding insult to injury, the first (and only, as it'd turn out) instalment of Korine's acting fee came through no more than five weeks after I'd terminated the Aldersgate Street subtenancy. I didn't expect it: surely, he could have found a way to open another bank account in my name, or ask my agent to delay payment until further notice: something, anything. But he didn't. I regretted, bitterly, that I'd got rid of the flat, leaving him at a loose end. I was – we were – living the consequences of my decision. I emailed the sublessor trying to rectify my mistake. He didn't reply so I phoned him. It was too late: a new subtenant had been found. Such was the rental market in EC1, he said, pretend regretfully, stating the obvious. On a positive note, I transferred Korine's money into Laurie's account in addition to my monthly contribution, without any explanation as to where it came from. 'We'll spend it on sandals for the boy,' I said, jokingly. 'Not even funny,' Laurie replied. At no point was I naive enough to think that Korine's reason for stalking me was the money I owed him.

That I could repay him what was his and he'd leave me alone. If only it were that simple.

That evening, I retrieved the OTF knife I'd duct-taped to the back of the wardrobe in my room. Weighing it in my hand, it felt fairly light yet sturdy. I noted that my relationship to it had changed: holding it felt reassuring. Empowering, even. I operated the spring mechanism by flicking the switch at the top of the handle: as before, the blade opened impressively quickly. Lively spring action, they called it online. I attempted jabbing motions. Thrusts, forward and up. This just in theory. It wasn't like I hadn't handled every imaginable prop – switchblades, pistols, machine guns – during various shoots and live performances in the past: how was this different. I retracted the blade using the slider at the side of the handle. Then I slipped the knife into the right pocket of my jean jacket. I checked myself in the mirror. With a subtle movement of my hand inside the pocket, I could either conceal the weapon or show its outline through the fabric, as the situation required. I didn't intend to use it. But I would carry it with me for the time being, see how I went. At the very least, it would bolster my confidence. Act as a deterrent, if need be. In the eventuality, I would be prepared.

Yet over the subsequent couple of weeks I did not see nor hear from Korine. His unexpected disengagement was in many ways worse than his offensive had been. What was he planning. What was he waiting for. I started looking over my shoulder. Double-locking the front door: not the first time he'd let himself in. I was on high alert twenty-four-seven, was nervy and getting into my head. It did not go unnoticed. We'd just gone into September: I was yet again on the balcony, keeping an eye on unwanted activity in the garden and bordering foliage (the wind the wind the heavenly child; a rat or a blue tit), when Laurie asked if we could talk. Absent-mindedly, I invited her to sit on one of the camping chairs. I'd stay where I was if she didn't mind, arms propped on the balcony railing, looking out. I was distracted, Laurie said, after a pause, and increasingly unreliable. My head was elsewhere. Really, she hadn't the faintest idea what I was up to half the time. Neither, and this was the worst part, did she know who I was. If I could drop the Korine charade. If I could stop with the Korine mannerisms and related BS. (She called it BS.) She'd been waiting for me to talk Aubrey Lewis, that is, my own past, my personal wins and losses. If I could let myself be known, as

Aubrey, I would give us a chance. Could I do that? Was I capable of it?

Before I could reassure her (just then, a movement of light in the reeds called for my attention), Laurie proceeded to moot the idea of me moving out. I wasn't her husband, Kirstie wasn't my child. I had no obligations towards either of them and neither did she towards me. No bad blood, no hard feelings. It wasn't like we hadn't tried.

What followed wasn't pretty. Finally turning to face her, I begged her to let me stay. To at least give me Mallorca. To give Kirstie Mallorca: six more sleeps, he was counting. We owed it to him, and to us. I'd be better. I'd stop doing what I was doing, I promised. I'd redeem myself.

'It's almost over,' I said. 'Not long now.' I wasn't sure what I meant by that.

Subsequently, I held myself to the promise I'd made to Laurie. I'd told her it was almost over, ergo I had to do something to end it. I couldn't tolerate the ongoing standoff between Korine and myself any longer either: I'd do anything to disrupt it. So I resolved to deal with him. First, I had to find him. Where to look? He was no longer in the flat on Aldersgate Street which, in this context, was a relief: I couldn't have brought myself to set foot in the place. The set of *As If*? They were shooting at Pinewood Studios, Iver Heath, I'd seen it announced on social media. But facing Korine amid TV professionals including my former colleagues? I'd rather not. What else: Korine struck me as a man with routines. A man who, if he did something once, would do it again: not unlike myself, for that matter. On that basis, I decided to visit Ludo's cafe. I would go tomorrow: Korine was filming during the week, but chances were, he'd be there on a Saturday: I would be, if I were him.

I'd have to proceed with caution: I would attend, not as myself, but in disguise. If the encounter went wrong, if it produced any unwanted outcomes, none of it could be traced back to me: I'd deny I was there. On an existential level, I feared the effects that a first-hand interaction with Korine would have on me. He was getting to me at the deepest, most personal level and I wasn't prepared to go anywhere near him without a degree of separation in place.

I could have chosen any disguise. But in an attempt to give my performance coherence, and/or as the result of an industry joke, namely that there were certain physical similarities between him and me, I decided to go as the second-rate actor Lucien Jelley. Personally, I'd never seen the resemblance. But in the absence of the time and resources required to develop a more elaborate role, I knew I could deliver a passable Jelley.

That afternoon – Laurie was at work or with her partner Sally, she was always with Sally these days, and Kirstie was back at school – I put on a pair of loafers I'd found in Korine's wardrobe a while ago, the sort Jelley would wear. I clipped a small silver earring to my left ear. (I would realise later that Jelley's earring was on the right.) Best of all, I found a black pair of trousers which I cut off above the ankles and paired with white socks. I practised his nasal intonation and the way he tended to push his tongue against the back of his front teeth until I executed the combined effect perfectly. I spent the following hours checking myself in the mirror, fine-tuning his mannerisms, until I was confident I was delivering a credible character.

I arrived at noon the following day, in full Jelley regalia. First impressions, Ludo's hadn't changed since early June, why would it, it hadn't in years. I made for my usual table and sat down. I had some insecurities around the jean jacket I had on which didn't seem like something Jelley would choose: he was the blazer- or suit-jacket-wearing type. It didn't take long until Korine walked through the door. He was wearing a pink cap with a neck flap and sunglasses. Despite his headgear, I could tell it was him. He was in worse shape than ever: worse than when first I met him in my flat; worse even than when last I saw him on my balcony. His trousers were torn and stained. His trainers – some old-man brand – were in half-decent shape, in contrast to his wax jacket which was covered in I didn't know what. I was aware I was partly responsible: I'd made him homeless. But he didn't look like a gainfully employed actor, or indeed anyone who had places to be.

Here we go, I thought and, alarmingly, what now. I'd been so preoccupied – distracted? – perfecting my Jelley that I had failed to establish what I would do once Korine showed up. Should I accost him? What would I say? What would a tête-à-tête really achieve? Meanwhile, Korine, who'd been scanning the room for a seat, stopped in his tracks. Noticing me, he made straight for my table – which caught me off-guard.

'May I?' he said, already pulling out the free chair from under the table. He didn't smell of fresh flowers exactly.

'Suit yourself,' I said, pretend casually. I half got up to greet him, then sat back down once he did. Internally, I was reeling: had he seen through my disguise? The jean jacket: a dead giveaway?

'Jelley,' Korine said, pronouncing the name like he despised it. He took off his sunglasses, looking me right in the eye. 'Fancy seeing you here.'

Korine knows Jelley, was all I could think. And then, at least my disguise is working, and then again, Korine and Jelley? How! At no point had I suspected there was any connection between the two. As far as I'd been concerned, they were strangers. What's more, Korine's hostility towards Jelley was let's say undisguised.

'And who do I have the pleasure with?' I came out with, staying in character. If Korine knew Jelley, it didn't follow that Jelley knew Korine. The latter could be a critic, armchair variety, or a disappointed fan, in other words a member of the public with feelings towards Jelley's let's call it acting oeuvre.

Korine didn't respond, not verbally. Instead, he rose from his chair and grabbed me by the collar. Then he launched into a tirade against me: the impertinence I possessed turning up in his local. After I'd swanned in and replaced him, had I no conscience.

After I'd taken everything he'd worked so hard to build. Had I no morals. Where was my integrity. He tightened his grip and pulled me towards the edge of the table. I resisted, bracing my hands against it, kicking my legs, eventually landing a loafer against his shin. He grimaced with pain, but didn't let up. By now, everybody was looking. The waiter who must've replaced Ludo had his hand on the panic button. Hovering. Ready to push. Suddenly, Korine moved sideways and, employing his hip, toppled the table between us. Cutlery went flying. Sugar dispenser, brown sauce and ketchup bottles were rolling across the floor like bowling pins. The patrons got up as one: napkins fell from laps or were hastily thrown onto half-finished plates. Without the table to protect me, Korine pulled me close, still clenching my collar, shoving me backwards through the room until I hit the wall. People had moved towards the counter or, if within reach, the door. Korine called me a thief, shaking me, and at that moment, the knife fell out of my pocket and onto the floor, clanging. He saw it and, reaching for it, loosened his hold on me. I slid down the wall and kicked the weapon across the floor. We both went after it. Somehow, pushing him to the side, flinging myself forward and onto the lino, I got there first. I swiped up the knife, made for the exit and legged it. Looking back as I ran, I saw Korine limp the other way, down Theobalds Road. I heard incoming sirens.

I retired Jelley with immediate effect. Turning into Clerkenwell Road, I removed the silly earring as quickly as I could. The loafers were next: neither had offered the least bit of protection. I threw the lot onto a pile of rubbish bags by the side of the road and continued in socks. How Korine knew Jelley, I'd never know. It didn't matter: he had double-bluffed me, going along with the Jelley charade to confuse or even ridicule me, knowing perfectly well it was me all along. Then, unconcealed violence: if this was what he was prepared to do in public, I thought, what would he do if he got hold of me in a dark corner of the estate. What would he do if he allowed himself.

I didn't sleep that night. I lay in my bed, hearing Laurie downstairs, packing a suitcase to take to Mallorca. Today I'd come closer to Korine than ever before. I had to admit to myself that, as much as I feared and resented him, I also envied him. He was a force, and I didn't just mean his physicality: he was more himself than I was, more than I'd ever be, which was ironic given the fact he had been impersonating me for months. I felt inadequate in comparison: this wasn't about the altercation earlier. It wasn't even about him being Lindsey Korine, Laurie's husband, Christ, Kirstie's father: this was going deeper and further back. When first he arrived at my flat, he had owned the place instantly. He had literally made it his own. He never questioned his right to be there, I mean, *I* did, the subtenant. Same thing in the cafe earlier: however reprehensible, Korine knew what he wanted and he went for it, no holds barred. Whereas I had lost myself a long time ago, and not just once. First, when I domesticated acting and settled for my role in *People*. Then again when I lost my wife and, alongside her, what little I had left of my so-called purpose. Even now, where Laurie and Kirstie were concerned, I was failing to get a purchase on anything real. I wondered what Laurie, my wife, would make of it all. I really missed her.

A suitcase and bags had appeared in the hallway. Among them, Kirstie's backpack with the monkey inside and two or three books. The plane to Mallorca would leave at eleven fifteen which meant there was time. If I left now, I could do what had to be done. No half measures, I promised myself. I picked up my jean jacket, the OTF knife in its pocket a permanent fixture by now.

'I'll be back,' I called at the door. 'Won't be long.'

'I've heard that one before,' Laurie said, more to Sally who she was on the phone with than to me.

I turned out of the entrance block and headed straight down Golden Lane for the Barbican underpass. I'd long since decided that's where I'd find him when the time came: where else would a person take shelter around here: I myself had ended up there, had I not. Clouds coming in from the north, I noted. It might rain later. The thought came to me that even now I could disengage. I didn't need to go through with it. In a few hours, we would be in Mallorca. First thing on arrival, I would take off my jean jacket. It, everything in it, would disappear into the suitcase for the duration of the stay. I imagined myself standing at the beach, watching Kirstie's head bop among the waves. One of his armbands had deflated: he was going round in circles as a result. Laurie was lying in a deckchair behind me, enjoying the peace. Who said we would return to London. We could stay. Start over. Rebuild on the island. But no sooner did I give in to a feeling of optimism than I got the sense that Korine was in my daydream too. As I scanned the vicinity, I saw he was lying on a beach towel mere yards away, cultivating a sunburn. He appeared to be reading, but, on closer inspection, he held the book – *As If*, as it were – upside down. This was how I knew he was watching me, waiting to corner me in a dark alley or behind that rock formation over there when least I expected it. I'd seen fishermen grab octopi by the tentacles and sling them against the surface of rocks just like these: a traditional, merciful way of killing. As I passed Fortune Street Park to my left, I let go of the notion that I had a choice in the matter. Korine was coming for me and there would be no letting up.

I saw him as soon as I turned into the underpass. He was alone, serenading no one in particular. When I say serenading I mean delivering a monologue, what was that from. I recognised it, but couldn't place it. He was formidable. A sight to behold. He was waving his awful arms and dragging his leg. He was somewhere else and yet, monitoring his reflection in the light blue panel in front of him, completely present. I couldn't help being moved seeing someone, Korine, act with the unpolished fervour of someone who gave it their all. How good he'd got, I thought, in a relatively short space of time. And how good would he get if he kept going.

A group of unsupervised schoolchildren went by. One or two slowed down to watch him, whispering behind covered mouths, giggling. They started heckling. Incomprehensibly, the smallest one started singing a Christmas carol, 'Merrily my heart shall leap', while the others stepped up their abuse. Meanwhile, I noticed the cars going past had their headlights on: it must've started to rain. They carried the wetness in on their tyres, leaving dark streaks on lighter asphalt.

I stepped closer. The children spotted me and, pointing, expressed their delight: two of them! they cried, there are two of them! They promptly started picking small pebbles from the pavement – construction detritus – which they proceeded to throw in my direction. Korine, implacable, continued soliloquising: once more with feeling, he didn't hold back. Then, unexpectedly, still facing the wall, he let his head fold forward and fell silent: like someone had pushed the off button. This was enough to attract renewed attention from the kids: they left me alone and started pelting the back of Korine instead. If he knew he was targeted he didn't show it: the projectiles rebounded from his tweed coat, tightly woven, or the wax jacket he was wearing on top: it was as if he were invincible.

Failing to provoke a reaction, the children got bored and drifted away. 'Merrily' and so on still filling the air when Korine turned around and sat down on the pavement. I took this as my cue to approach.

'May I?' I asked.

'Lewis!' His eyes widened as he recognised me.

I sat down without waiting for his permission. For a while, we sat next to each other, eerily calmly, backs against the beige panelling, legs pulled up, allowing the occasional passer-by to pass by, all was right in the world on that front at least. The apex of his knees was higher than mine, his head an inch above, but when it came down to it, there really wasn't much between us. I wondered who would make the first move: Korine or myself. I was prepared either way. My right hand went into my pocket. Grip first relaxed, then tightening around the knife's handle.

Seeing him this close up, looking into the whites of his eyes, I could've seen him for what he was: his own person, with his own life, his own struggles. I did and I didn't. I didn't in the sense that I saw something in him that I felt drawn to but that I'd defended against my entire adulthood. It, he, constituted a threat so real, so substantial, it needed containing at all costs.

I shifted my hand to the edge of my pocket, just enough for me to release the blade: a soft click as I did. I looked to my right without moving my head. His left temple like a bullseye, the easiest target on earth.

Then, unexpectedly, he put his head on my shoulder. Let it fall as if naturally to the side. That moment, he looked like the saddest living being in the world, sitting there with those arms of his, hugging his legs. His pointy elbows, it was pitiful. In a sense, he looked like I felt: as if he'd experienced a colossal loss. As an actor, I appreciated the silliness of the word pairing: colossal loss. Those words were not meant to appear anywhere near each other, never mind next to each other, least of all from an enunciation point of view. I couldn't help but pity Korine which, if he were playing me, might be precisely where he wanted me: I hesitated, perhaps to my detriment.

I asked him what kept him alive.

'Acting,' he said. He wanted to get better at it, and

this aspiration, this hope, kept him going day after day after day. He followed this up by asking why *I* bothered. What kept me going.

I thought about Laurie, my wife, the fact that I'd known her, and Korine's wife. I thought about Kirstie. I thought about acting, too, and I didn't mean the professionalised, defanged version I'd become overfamiliar with. I didn't mean playing Korine either, which, I finally realised, represented this exact sort of acting at best: the Schmidt of this year. I meant *acting*: playing Simon in an imaginary production of *Lord of the Flies*. Playing Vladimir in *Godot*. Playing Colin in *The Loneliness of the Long Distance Runner* and, even more so, failing at it. And by playing Simon, Vladimir, Colin I didn't mean playing the lead in a major production. I meant playing a role, any role, like it mattered. An image came to me of the child actor I once was, who entertained the sports shop's clientele against their wishes. Who got bullied at school for simply rehearsing. Who wasn't encouraged by anyone, but who insisted on himself with an urgency I'd not known since. This risk-to-life-and-limb sort of actor: who could he be at forty-six, naivety lost, seasoned. The point was, I didn't know. I'd never dared to find out.

He had an audition lined up the following week, Korine said. Small talking part, mid-budget production. He had to start somewhere. (Me: 'What happened to *As If*?' Korine: 'It wasn't for me.') He was going to rebuild from the ground up. Make a name for himself: his own name, Lindsey Korine. 'Call-out fits your description, too, Lewis. Middle-aged Caucasian male. 40–50y. £120 day fee. Travel expenses paid.'

'I might go for it,' I said, meaning it. 'Do you mind.'

'Open season,' he said.

I didn't respond. I could land the knife in the side of his neck with force if I wanted to. I thought about it. I did. But instead, I nudged his head off my shoulder and got up. I walked to the kerb. Then I pulled the knife out of my pocket and dropped it into the sewer. It took two attempts: final push, tip of my foot.

'What was that,' Korine asked.

'Nothing,' I said. Not important.

He said not to patronise him.

I said to shut up. I sat back down.

'What time is it,' I asked after a while. Laurie and Kirstie must be about to leave for the airport.

He had no idea what time it was. So we sat in silence.

I said I was cold. In fact, I felt a wind chill coming from my right as if I were unprotected on that side. As if there weren't an extra-tall person to hide behind.

As it happened, Korine said, he was wearing double layers. Thick layers, too. No flimsy jean jacket. 'Want one?'

'Yes,' I said. 'Yes.'

And when I turned to accept his spare jacket, which felt like I was sealing my so-called fate, one of the passing cars had its headlights on full beam, dazzling me, and I thought for a mad split second that there was nobody there.

Acknowledgements

Thanks to Simon Prosser, Hermione Thompson and Ruby Fatimilehin at Hamish Hamilton.

Thanks to Katie Cacouris at The Wylie Agency in New York, and special thanks to Tracy Bohan at Wylie in London.

Thanks to Milo Walls at Farrar, Straus & Giroux.

Thanks to my readers.

Thanks, always, to Lisa Blackman.